The window exploded

McCarter's form was briefly outlined with the flying debris of wood and glass splinters, then he saw the surface of the flat roof rushing to meet him, and he relaxed his body, allowing it to curl up loosely as he struck the roof. He rolled, absorbing the impact, then slithered to a stop.

He had regained his feet in a semicrouch and was just starting to wonder about pursuit when the harsh crackle of automatic fire opened up. Hot slugs blasted chunks of black tar into the air around him. It was a definite encouragement to hotfoot it, McCarter thought as he propelled himself into a zigzag course.

Mack Bolan's
PHOENIX FORCE.

PHOENIX FORCE.

GAR WILSON

MISSILE MENACE

A GOLD EAGLE BOOK FROM

WORLDWIDE.

TORONTO • NEW YORK • LONDON • PARIS
AMSTERDAM • STOCKHOLM • HAMBURG
ATHENS • MILAN • TOKYO • SYDNEY

First edition November 1988

ISBN 0-373-61338-5

Special thanks and acknowledgment to
Mike Linaker for his contribution to this work.

Printed in U.S.A.

PROLOGUE

Salisbury Plain, England

Kovic led the assault on the perimeter guards. There were four armed soldiers to be taken out. It was an easy task for Kovic and his team. The job was done swiftly. Efficiently. And in complete silence.

The moment Kovic's signal reached him, Manson moved in with the rest of the group. They filed through the opened gates of the compound, each man moving toward his assigned task without further orders.

The night was still and silent, lit by a soft moon, and it was warm. Warm enough to have lulled the senses of the combined United States-British Army unit on duty within the compound. They had been on this assignment for almost a month now. It was easy duty, maybe too easy, because it had started to get boring. And a bored soldier can easily become a dead soldier.

They were housed in a low, prefabricated building tacked on to the longer vehicle parking garage.

Manson reached the prefab. He paused, his .45-caliber Detonics Automatic cocked and ready in his right hand, then raised his left hand and opened the door. As he stepped into the room, he moved to the left of the door, leaving the way clear for the others to follow.

There were five men in the room. From the look of their uniforms three were American, and the other two were British. They all glanced up as Manson entered.

"Attention!" Manson ordered loudly, aware of the instinctive reaction of the trained military mind.

Three of the soldiers sprung to their feet. Of the remaining two, one simply raised his eyes from the magazine he was holding and just stared. The fifth man, an American captain, took a longer look. It only lasted for a few seconds, and he didn't like what he saw.

He did see men dressed in U.S. Army uniforms. But he also saw Uzi submachine guns. An Ingram MAC-10. None were standard U.S. Army issue.

He also sensed a menacing air about these men, and instinctively knew they were the enemy.

The captain began to get up from his chair, trying to make the move as natural as possible. At the same time he reached for the M-16 propped against the wall by his chair. He knew he was stretching the odds, but he had to try. It was his duty, and he'd never shirked that before.

His fingers touched the M-16, gripped it, and he began to lift it.

A split second passed, just enough for him to realize that he'd made a fatal mistake, but he kept on with it. There was no other choice.

Manson fired first, the Detonics .45 thundering loudly, spitting out its heavy bullet with shattering force. It ripped its way into the captain's skull just above the left eye, plowing through the brain to emerge from the back of his head.

As the captain was slammed against the wall, staining it with his spurting blood, Kovic, who had entered right after Manson, caught a glimpse of one of the soldiers lunging off to the side. Kovic arced the muzzle of his Ingram around, lining it up on target. He touched the trigger and sent half a magazine ripping through the man's body. The burst of slugs tore the torso open in a misty splatter of blood and shredded flesh. Splintered bone gleamed white against the pulsing slick of blood. Tossed across the room by the force of the bullets, the soldier crashed against a table, overturning it in a mess of books, loose-leaf papers and plastic cups.

The man's death throes distracted Manson. He stood over the dying man and put a single .45 slug through his head, ending the writhing.

"Any more heroes?" Kovic asked pointedly, the Ingram tracking from man to man.

The survivors tore their gaze from the shredded remains of their two former companions and became instantly passive.

"Landis, fix the radio," Manson ordered.

Landis moved to the communications set and cut its power.

"You three, facedown on the floor," Manson said.

As the soldiers obeyed, Kovic secured their hands behind their backs with plastic riot handcuffs.

"All right, breathe easy for a minute," Manson said. He glanced at the sweating Kovic. "Relax, Ron. We've done it."

Kovic's wide brutish face fixed him with a scowl. "It'll be done when we hand over those trucks. Until then I ain't takin' one easy breath!"

Manson grinned. "Hey, Landis, keep an eye on the prisoners. Ron, let's go take a look at what we've got. Might make you feel better."

The compound outside was busy as Manson's team opened the doors of the garages. Inside were four identical thirty-foot trailers, each pulled by a diesel tractor. The cab of each tractor had been extended by some eight feet, making a compact operating unit. The flatbed trailers were covered by half-cylindrical shells. The four rigs were all painted in dull Army livery.

Manson stood for a moment, running his gaze almost lovingly over the units. Then he waved to the waiting men. "Let's go. Get these things out of here."

He turned to Kovic and punched him lightly on one muscular arm. "We're out of here, Ron."

The night's silence was broken by the throaty roar of four diesel engines bursting into life. One by one the rigs eased out of the sheds, rolled across the compound and rumbled off into the darkness.

Kovic summoned Landis from the prefab and sent him from the compound. Then he glanced inquiringly at Manson. "Well?"

Manson returned his stare. "We leave no one who can identify us," he said.

Kovic nodded and put a fresh magazine in the Ingram, then turned and trotted to the prefab. Moments later the weapon crackled as Kovic used the full magazine on the helpless prisoners. As the last echoes of gunfire drifted away, Kovic rejoined Manson.

They walked out of the silent compound and followed the dusty trail left by the four rigs. Shortly Landis drove up in the four-wheel drive Honda they had arrived in. Kovic took over the wheel, Manson hopped in beside him, and Landis got in the back and seated himself at the radio so he could monitor any transmissions that might affect them.

"Move out, Sergeant Kovic," Manson said, smiling easily. He was pleased with the night's work, and his precise planning.

Phase one of the operation was complete, and within a few days phase two would commence.

Manson considered what would come after that, then shrugged, accepting that despite their planning for every contingency, things could go against them. This far-reaching operation, like everything else in life, was a gamble. A pessimist would look at the odds and say there was a fifty percent chance of failure. Manson, always a gambler and optimist, figured the opposite. A fifty percent chance of succeeding was well worth gambling on. And the more he thought about it, the clearer it became that the odds were all in his favor.

He had already turned his back on the country of his birth, and that marked him for death. So if he lost the game he was playing and ended up a dead man, then nothing else would matter anyway.

But if the operation was a success he would be an extremely wealthy and powerful man. And that meant everything to Alex Manson.

Just the thought of power excited him. Manson had always been aware of the elusive narcotic effect of power. The need for it had always been with him, and his career in the United States Army had given him some degree of authority over others, had given him a taste—but never enough. Power generated a need for more power. It was something that Alex Manson craved. A controlled desire for it, coupled with a natural talent for leadership, had pushed him steadily through the ranks to the captaincy. His keen brain had kept him alert to possibilities to further his position, yet somehow his military advancement had halted, and Manson had realized eventually that he wasn't going to get any higher. It was a blow. Disappointment gave way to bitterness, which in turn bred disenchantment with the Army and with a country that had failed to recognize his worth. His demand for personal achievement grew in proportion to his evident failure to obtain more, and it became his total preoccupation. It dominated his thoughts and actions, and in his mind he feverishly sought fresh avenues toward the pursuit of that end.

It was around then that the Russian called Lubichek had come into his life. Lubichek was with the KGB—something Manson hadn't learned until later. But that had made no difference because Lubichek had offered Manson the one guaranteed thing to gain his loyalty.

The promise of power.

Manson sold his services willingly. He wasn't overly concerned about selling out his country. Loyalty was something he reserved for his own ideals, not for some vague ideological claptrap. A man was born and lived and died. In the period between birth and death he had one chance at individual greatness. Lubichek had offered Manson that opportunity, and as far as Manson was concerned, it wouldn't have mattered if the offer had come from Lenin himself. The "who" didn't concern Manson. He was simply interested for himself. He saw the main chance coming his way, and he was determined to grab the brass ring.

When Lubichek had revealed his scheme, Manson had been briefly stunned by its audacity. It was far

bigger, wider reaching than he could have anticipated. But he quickly grasped the overall effect, and
the irony of it appealed to him.

It was grand strategy at its best. The ultimate outrage. The consequences were staggering: they might
even trigger world conflict, topple democracy and in-
stigate total anarchy.

And he, ex-Captain Alex Manson, would be part of
it. As far as he was concerned, that was the best part
of the "who" deal.

1

It didn't pay, David McCarter thought as he sat in a corner of the pub, sipping his Coke. Going back was a mistake, because everything changed with time. People and places. Nothing was the same anymore. He stared around the smoky, crowded pub, and didn't feel a damn thing.

He'd been wrong coming back, even if it was for just a short visit. He should have stayed up in the West End of London, at his hotel, where he could have had a good meal and an early night before catching the plane back to the U.S. in the morning. Instead, he had driven down to the East End to the Dog and Partridge, one of his old haunts from his SAS days. Why he'd done it, he wasn't sure. Whatever his motives had been, the justification for them had failed to materialize.

The pub showed no sign of alterations from the outside, and the interior decoration hadn't been improved by age. The Dog and Partridge stood on the corner of a narrow side street, just off the Mile End Road. For a brief moment, as he paused outside, McCarter had experienced a vivid recall of the feel of those long-gone days. Then he had pushed in through the door. Although it looked pretty well the same, something was missing. It was the atmosphere. And there were none of the old faces. Even the landlord was new—a younger man with a lean, hungry face. The barmaids were a different breed, too. All youngsters. Too much makeup and not enough clothing. McCarter had ordered a can of Coke, for which he had paid an exorbitant price, and had threaded his way through the crowd to a small table in one corner of the pub. He sat and sipped the cold drink. Oh well, you silly bugger, it serves you right! he chided himself.

David McCarter had flown to England two days before. He'd taken a few days R and R to attend the funeral of an ex-SAS buddy who had died in a car accident. McCarter had shared a few hectic times with the man during his service days, and it seemed right and proper to attend his burial. Back in London after the funeral, McCarter had become slightly bored through inactivity and had made the mistake of allowing himself some reminiscing. Hence his arrival in the East End and the visit to the Dog and Partridge.

He dug a packet of Player's from his pocket and was about to light one when he caught sight of a familiar face at the bar.

"Well," the Briton muttered, "if it isn't Jake Tasker!" He stood up and called, "Hey Jake. Over here, mate, and make it snappy. I'm dying of boredom!"

The man at the bar had turned his way. For a moment it seemed as though he might dash out, but then he picked up his pint glass of beer and made his way to McCarter's table. "Hello, David," Tasker said as he sat down. "It's been a long time."

"Too bloody long," McCarter said with a grin. Then he took in Tasker's pale hard-set features and caught the look in the man's eyes. Immediately he knew that something was really wrong.

It was mirrored in Tasker's frightened stare and in the way he held himself. Tasker seemed so tense, as though he would explode at any moment, and David McCarter seemed to be the most likely one to catch the blast.

Not that the possibility worried him. He had seen a lot of action as a member of Phoenix Force, the U.S. commando squad, and one man's displeasure didn't worry him. McCarter was not a man given to sitting around and doing a great deal of thinking. He liked action and was always ready and eager to jump in with both feet. Some people got their kicks from drink, others from drugs. David McCarter got his from being in the thick of the action. He craved excitement with the enthusiasm of a small boy longing for candy. McCarter was never better than when he was knee-deep in a physical confrontation, and the higher the odds, the better he liked it.

Sensing his old friend's distress, McCarter reacted instantly. He put down his soft drink and put away his cigarettes. "All right, Jake, let's have it. What's wrong?"

"Eh?" Tasker gulped down the remainder of his beer. "*Wrong?* Nothing, David, nothing."

"Come off it, Jake, I know you too well. And I can recognize somebody who's frightened. Now come on and cut out the bullshit."

Tasker stared hard at McCarter and understood that he had a friend who wanted to help.

"Do you have a car?" he asked.

McCarter nodded. "Hire job around the corner."

"Can you get me away from here?"

"No problem. Just leave it to me."

McCarter stood. He took Tasker's arm and guided him through the pub to a door marked Toilets. They went through. A short passage led to the rest rooms, with an exit door at the far end. McCarter shoved it open, and he and Tasker found themselves in a dimly lit alley at the side of the pub. The door swung shut behind them, locking with a metallic click.

"This way," McCarter said, but Tasker wasn't listening. He was staring over McCarter's shoulder, his eyes wide with undisguised fear. McCarter spun around to search for the object of fear, and saw them.

Three of them. Young, lean and hard faced.

They looked to be muggers who had been waiting for someone to leave by the side door. Waiting for a chance to jump some poor drunken soul. Kick their victim to the ground, beat him senseless, then rob him.

All right, boys, McCarter thought, come and try it with me.

He eased by Tasker, and let the three punks come at him.

They came in a sudden rush. There was no organization. No unified movement. Simply an uncoordinated, blind rush.

McCarter let them close in before he made his first move. His right fist drove forward and up in a short, devastating punch that caught the guy in the center of his neck. The man fell back, his eyes bulging. He lost his balance and crashed to the ground where he lay writhing in pain, unable to utter a sound because McCarter's knuckles had damaged his vocal cords and windpipe.

In the moment it took him to deliver the blow McCarter half turned, bringing himself in line with the second mugger. He easily blocked an ill-timed punch aimed at his stomach and countered with his left hand, the palm smashing up under the man's vulnerable, unshaved jaw. The mugger's head rocked back sharply, his teeth snapping together with force. The brutal impact of the blow sent the mugger spinning across the alley and slammed him up against the grimy brick wall. The back of his skull impacted against the wall, bouncing him off and pitching him facedown on the ground.

McCarter faced the last attacker. The fox-faced Briton was just starting to warm up, and beginning to enjoy himself.

The third mugger, somewhat stunned by what had happened, glanced about as if he was looking for a way out. He realized there wasn't one. The only way of escape was blocked by David McCarter.

"Come on, chum, see if you can do better than your pals!" McCarter taunted. "Try your luck, scumbag. It'd be a miracle if you could take an old lady in a wheelchair."

The mugger's face flushed with anger. He was letting hurt pride dictate his actions. It was a mistake, but just what McCarter had wanted to happen.

"Get out of my way!" the punk yelled, then stabbed a finger in Tasker's direction. "You shouldn't have interfered. We only wanted him."

With a slight hesitation the mugger reached under **his leather jacket and dragged out a Korth .357 Com**bat Magnum that had a silencer screwed to the barrel. "I'll kill you both!" the would-be assassin yelled.

While he was threatening, McCarter was on the move. He ducked in low, under the descending gun barrel, and his right shoulder slammed into the guy's stomach. There was a choking gasp, followed by the soft *phutt* of the silenced revolver. McCarter felt the punk backpedal. They crashed against the alley wall. Reaching up to grab the guy's wrist and keep the gun out of the way, McCarter knotted the fingers of his right hand in his opponent's thick hair. He slammed the head back, cracking the guy's skull against the wall a couple of times, and the moment he felt his adversary sag a little McCarter yanked the head forward and down. As the limp form started to pitch forward, McCarter jerked his right knee upward. The descending face met the ascending knee with savage force. The man grunted once and dropped to the ground, his face streaming blood. As he went down, McCarter slipped the revolver from the unresisting fingers.

Kneeling beside the limp figure, McCarter swiftly searched him. All he found was a thick wad of twenty-pound notes; there must have been at least five thousand pounds in the roll. There were also a couple of .357-caliber quick-loaders. McCarter ignored the money but put away the ammo. The rest of the pockets were empty. A similar search of the other two men resulted in the same thing—plenty of cash, nothing else.

The fact that all three were carrying large amounts of cash removed any suspicion that the attack had been simply an attempted mugging. It just didn't ring true as far as David McCarter was concerned.

Muggers wouldn't carry so much cash around; if they had so much there hardly seemed any point for them to try any further. Also, petty thieves of that type seldom carried guns—and especially an expensive weapon like the Korth. The silencer took the game a step higher. Ordinary street thugs didn't go in for sophisticated gadgets like silencers.

Nothing, McCarter decided, was adding up correctly. Two and two kept coming out five. The way things were stacking up the attack had to have been an attempted murder disguised as a street mugging.

The next question was, why? What had Tasker gotten involved in to bring on an attempt on his life? McCarter didn't know the answer to that yet—but he was determined to find out.

2

A soft groan made McCarter turn.

Jake Tasker was slumped against the pub wall, his right hand gripping his left wrist. Blood oozed from between his fingers.

"You hit bad?" McCarter asked.

"Just clipped me," Tasker said from between clenched teeth.

McCarter shoved the gun in his waistband. "Come on. My car is just around the corner."

The rental car was a black Ford Sierra. McCarter unlocked the doors and made sure Tasker was settled. Then he slipped behind the wheel and started the car. He put it in gear and cruised along the narrow street until he reached the junction and turned on to the Mile End Road.

"Where to, Jake?"

"The Ridgeway Hotel off the Bayswater Road," Tasker said. "I've been hanging out there for a week."

"Okay, guv, Bayswater it is," McCarter said in his best Cockney accent.

It was close on nine-thirty and getting dark. McCarter was familiar with the London Streets and drove nonstop. Even so it took a good twenty minutes to reach the hotel in Bayswater. He found an empty spot and parked the Sierra along the curb.

"Let's get inside," Tasker said.

The hotel was medium-size, one of a hundred similar types that were dotted around the Bayswater area. It had once been a fashionable residential neighborhood, but had then declined. The rows of colonnaded homes had been converted to rooming houses, and slow decay was apparent on the once white frontages.

The sleepy girl on the reception desk handed Tasker his key without a second glance and returned to watching the flickering black-and-white picture on a portable TV set in a corner of her office.

They took the stairs to Tasker's room on the third floor. Reaching the door, McCarter took the key and unlocked it. He fisted the Korth Magnum, edging the door open with his foot. The room was in darkness. McCarter checked it out before giving the all clear. Inside he flicked on the light, then closed and locked the door.

The first priority was Tasker's gouged wrist. The bullet had dug a furrow about a quarter inch deep across the top of his wrist. The edges of the wound were ragged but clean. McCarter nevertheless made Tasker hold his wrist under the tap in the bathroom to wash away the congealed blood. After inspecting the wound McCarter bound it with one of the small hand towels.

"Not bad, but you'd best get it looked at."

"Yeah," Tasked replied, but it was clear his mind wasn't on what he was saying.

"All right, fill me in," McCarter directed his friend.

Tasker slumped into a chair by the window. He suddenly looked very tired. "I seem to have found trouble, David."

"No doubt about it," McCarter said wryly.

Tasker leaned back, staring at a spot on the ceiling. "I moved to free-lance investigative journalism about eight years ago. I'd had enough working on provincial newspapers. I've done pretty well for myself since. Built a reputation. Had some strong articles in some of the major dailies. About three weeks ago I got a tip from a guy who often feeds me information. He said I should look into the affairs of a group calling themselves the RBP. My informant said these people were out to cause trouble.

"It all sounded a bit fancy, but you know what it's like when a reporter gets a whiff of a story. I did some checking. Used other informants. I found out that RBP stands for Red Britannia Party. It's a fanatic Communist cell composed of real hard-liners. Way to the left of the British Communist party. These guys would stand up and cheer if the Russkies declared war. I managed to get hold of their official manifesto. It advocates some really radical measures. These RBP guys are crazy, David. Real hotheads. But up to now they haven't done anything to break the law."

"That's the problem with democracy," McCarter said. "A nut case can stand up and shout from the rooftops about what he wants to do. But as long as he keeps to words he can get away with it."

"Well, from what I've learned about the RBP they may be intending to go one step further and actually do something."

"How did you find out?"

"Simple, really. I went to one of their meetings, trailed a few of them to a pub and watched out for the ones who liked their drink. When I spotted the one I wanted, I hung around until he was on his own, then latched on to him. It was smooth sailing after that. I told him I'd been to a couple of their meetings and I liked what they were advocating. It was all bullshit, of course, but this guy lapped it up. Like most of these radicals he loved to talk, and once I'd bought him a few more drinks he was really in the mood. I just let him get on with it. All I had to do was sit there and make the kind of noises he wanted to hear. He figured I was right for RBP, so I agreed.

"Then he started to get really creepy. He was talking about actual destruction, having the country in a big mess and the RBP stepping in and taking over. I wasn't certain he was genuine. But the way he talked scared the hell out of me. It was getting late by then. He was pretty tanked up. But his story stayed the same, so I really started to take notice. The last thing he said was 'Wait until the Manta falls.'"

"Manta? What's that?" McCarter asked.

"I don't know, because just then a couple of his buddies came into the pub hunting for him. They were looking mad. They carted him on out of there and told me to stay away from him. I don't think they knew who I was then. Anyway, the next day there was a story in one of the local papers about a guy falling under a tube train on the Piccadilly Line. They had a picture of this guy. It was the one I'd been talking to. I figured right off it was no accident.

"Right after that I found out I was being followed. And it wasn't my imagination, David, because I spotted one of the bastards. It was the same guy who'd told me to back off. The more I thought about it, the more it dawned on me that I'd got something. I needed time to build up my story, so I went to my place, threw some stuff in a bag and slipped out the back way. I spent hours crisscrossing London until I figured I'd lost any tail. Then I jumped a cab and booked in here.

"I've been here ever since. Writing up everything I know about the RBP and what the guy in the pub told me. By this afternoon I'd had enough. I didn't give a damn about those creeps looking for me. I just had to get out. I took a cab to the Dog and Partridge. I should have realized they'd look for me in my old stamping ground. Then you turned up." Tasker smiled. "You know the rest, David."

"The bad penny, that's me. Always in the wrong place at the right time."

"I just wish I'd been able to get more out of the guy in the pub."

"Let's not worry about that now. What we need to do is get you to somewhere safe. These RBP goons must have figured your drunken pal told you too much. They need to silence you. Sorry to be so blunt, but that's the way it looks to me." McCarter grinned. "There I was, thinking it was only me who got into trouble."

"I'd like to know more about this Manta, whatever it is," Tasker said.

"Me too, mate. And I may be able to find out something."

"How?"

McCarter tapped the side of his nose. "No can tell. But don't worry, if I find out anything you'll hear about it."

Tasker nodded. "Okay, I won't pry." He stood up and headed for the bathroom.

McCarter reached for the telephone and started to dial a number. He was going to try to get through to Hal Brognola, Phoenix Force's liaison with the White

House. The head federal agent would be at the Stony Man Farm headquarters in Virginia.

As Tasker reached out to flick on the bathroom light, there was a tap on the door. He turned toward it.

McCarter had heard the knock, as well, and began to turn his head to see Tasker reach the door and ask, "Yes?"

"Bloody hell, no!" McCarter yelled, flinging himself from the telephone. "Jake—down—"

His words were lost in a vicious burst of automatic gunfire. Bullets ripped hotly through the flimsy panel of the door, chewing their way into and through Jake Tasker's body. The impact of the slugs tossed Tasker back into the room amid a spray of blood. He hit the wall, twisting and turning before the sheer weight of his body dragged him to the floor.

Even as Tasker was falling, McCarter had dropped to the floor, so that stray bullets whined over his head to chew the plaster of the far wall. He pulled the Magnum from his belt, flicking the barrel up at the door. His finger tightened against the trigger, eased back and sent a .375 slug spinning through the upper panel. He was rewarded by the sound of a body hitting the floor on the other side of the door. Someone shouted in anger. A second burst of automatic fire crackled out. Splinters of wood flew across the room, showering down on McCarter. He twisted his body aside, hugging the wall. He had barely completed the move when the door burst open from a heavy impact.

A man plunged in through the opening with a stubby Ingram clutched in his hands. The gunman scanned the room, his eyes searching for a standing figure. In the time it took for him to lower his gaze,

McCarter fired twice. His first bullet found the man's neck, and the second blasted through his face, burrowing up through flesh and bone to destroy the brain. The man managed to take three more forward steps even as the top of his skull exploded outwards.

Not knowing if there were any more gunmen outside the room, McCarter decided to opt for the back way out. He lunged to his feet and flicked off the light switch. His gaze rested briefly on Tasker's body, and he saw there was nothing he could do for his journalist friend. Tasker had caught a half clip of slugs from the Ingram. His chest and face were a mess of chewed, ragged flesh and bone.

As the room darkened, McCarter turned and raced to the window. He yanked it open and peered out. To one side of the window a drainpipe snaked down to the ground. McCarter didn't hesitate. He thrust the Magnum into the waistband of his pants and clambered over the sill, reaching for the drainpipe. He felt it give a little and hoped it would support his weight. If it didn't, he was going to reach the ground in record time.

"Convince yourself you're Spiderman," he muttered. He tried, but he still felt distinctly vulnerable as he leaned his full weight on the pipe. McCarter went down hand over hand, not bothering to look up or down. His shoes skidded on the grimy brickwork as he tried to slow his rapid descent, and it was with some surprise that he reached the ground all in one piece. He snatched the Korth from his belt again, throwing a cautious glance up at Tasker's window.

A dark shape was leaning out. The illumination from a street lamp glanced off the dull metal of a gun. A split second later the gun opened up. Hot slugs splintered the sidewalk around McCarter's feet. He raised the Korth and loosed off two quick shots. He heard glass shatter and saw the enemy's quick retreat back into the room.

McCarter turned and ran along the side of the hotel. When he reached the frontage, he peered around the corner. His Sierra was where he'd left it. A few yards behind it was a pale blue Mercedes sedan. McCarter slipped the car key from his pocket, took a deep breath and dashed along the sidewalk toward the Sierra. He tried to keep one eye on the entrance to the hotel, and also watch for anyone in the Mercedes. It was only when he got to within a few yards of his rental car that he saw the lone guy in the luxury car's passenger seat. McCarter kept moving along the sidewalk to reach the driver's door of his vehicle. He had the key in the lock before the guy in the Mercedes became fully aware of him.

The guy yelled something and kicked open his door, lunging out of the Mercedes. He swung his right arm up, and lamplight bounced off the metal of a Browning automatic. But he never got a chance to use the weapon. McCarter's Korth chugged once, pitching the would-be killer in a lifeless pile onto the Mercedes's shiny paintwork and windshield.

McCarter scrambled behind the wheel, shoving the key in the ignition. The warm engine caught first time. Releasing the brake, he shoved the gearshift into first, flattened the accelerator and popped the clutch. The Sierra howled away from the curb, burning rubber all the way down the street. At the first intersection McCarter yanked the wheel around and took the bend at about fifty miles per hour. The Sierra protested but hugged the road. McCarter, grinning, kept up the high speed for the next two blocks. Then, certain that he wasn't being followed he eased off, not wanting to get stopped by the local police.

He cruised for the next quarter hour, trying to plan ahead. He needed to talk to Brognola at Stony Man headquarters. Whatever it was he'd walked into, for some reason he felt that it was big and needed handling by a larger force than one man. What it needed was Phoenix Force.

On the double.

A slow chuckle escaped from McCarter's lips. His homecoming was turning out to be a lot livelier than even he could have anticipated.

It proved one thing to McCarter.

There was a lot of life in the old country still!

3

Jake Tasker's apartment was on the third floor of a
terraced row in a quiet residential street in Hampstead, close to the Belsize Park Underground station.
The street had a rural charm with its neat houses and
spreading shade trees, and it was hard to believe it was
only a short distance from the heart of the city. Beyond the street, though, the neighborhood underwent
an abrupt change. Hampstead High Street was a busy
thoroughfare with shops, fast-food establishments and
even a movie theater.

David McCarter cruised his rental car along the
quiet street. He had decided to make an attempt to get
into Tasker's home, in case the journalist had left any
information there regarding his last assignment.
McCarter figured he might also be able to make his
interrupted telephone call to Hal Brognola.

The house he was looking for was at the far end of
the street. As McCarter neared the place, he spotted a
car parked outside and jammed on the Sierra's brakes,
bringing the car to a rocking halt.

"Blast my bloody luck!" the Briton mumbled.

The car outside Tasker's house was the same Mercedes that had parked outside the Ridgeway Hotel. It
seemed as though the opposition had beaten Mc-
Carter to Tasker's home.

McCarter's gaze was drawn to an upstairs window of the house. A moment later a sudden burst of orange and yellow flame erupted through the window, showering glass to the ground below.

McCarter gripped the steering wheel hard in sudden anger. Bang went another chance for him. The opposition was making certain there was no evidence left to point the finger at them. Whatever else they were, McCarter had to admit they were thorough.

Even as McCarter put the Sierra in reverse, he saw dark figures burst from the house and race for the Mercedes. He gunned the motor and spun the wheel, intending to make a rapid U-turn. As the car arced around McCarter caught a glimpse of the blue Mercedes. The lights were on and it suddenly surged forward. There was a screech of tires on the asphalt as the Mercedes took off at high speed.

McCarter swore vehemently, angry at himself. They'd recognized the car he was driving. Of all the stupid things to do! He'd gone and driven right up to them, almost advertising himself.

He pushed the pedal to the floor. He didn't slow down as he reached the end of the street but twisted the wheel to the left, taking the Sierra onto the main street.

Behind him the Mercedes followed suit, lurching around the corner with its rear end sliding.

McCarter settled back in his seat, a taut grin on his face. *All right, if it's fun and games you want, here goes!*

He hammered the Sierra along the High Street, making a straight run for Hampstead Heath itself. Shortly he was traveling along the road that passed through the expanse of wooded, grassy landscape. On the far side of the heath he cut across onto the A502, heading north. The Sierra's lights pierced brightly through the encroaching darkness. McCarter pushed the car as fast as he could, aware of the closeness of the pursuing Mercedes. He didn't want them getting too close, otherwise someone might open fire.

Approaching Golders Green McCarter suddenly cut over onto the Finchley Road, the Sierra rocking wildly at the abrupt change of direction. As he reached Henley's Corner, he swung left, tires protesting, onto the Great North Way. There was a trickle of cars about there, and McCarter had to do some sharp lane-switching in order to maintain his lead over the following car. Other drivers flashed their lights and sounded their horns at the black Sierra.

The Mercedes driver did his best to keep up, but he was not as skilled a driver as David McCarter—nor did he have the Phoenix warrior's cool nerves. McCarter rocked the hurtling vehicle about with nonchalant ease as he dodged between cars, enjoying every second of the hair-raising chase.

After a few more miles the Great North Way ran parallel to the M1, the country's major motorway, a three-lane freeway that ran from London all the way to Leeds in the north of England. This, McCarter decided, was the ideal place on which to lose his pursuers, and the moment he spotted the road heading to the motorway he took it.

With the entrance ramp falling rapidly behind him McCarter opened the Sierra up, watching the speedometer needle rise rapidly. The fixed speed limit on British motorways is seventy miles per hour. McCarter was already doing eighty when he left the slip road and merged onto the motorway. He jammed his foot down hard, sending the Sierra hurtling up the straight center lane, glad that the thinning traffic had diminished to nothing at that particular spot.

Throwing a hurried glance in the rearview mirror, McCarter spotted the unmistakable bulk of the Mercedes coming up fast on his rear. The German car obviously had a bigger-capacity engine than the Sierra, and it was eating up the distance between them fast. Too fast for McCarter's liking.

Time for a different tactic, he decided.

Steadily the Mercedes gained on McCarter's vehicle, coming up fast on his rear. McCarter let the Mercedes get to within a few yards, then he touched his brakes. The Ford slowed and the Mercedes driver, not reacting quickly enough, allowed his front bumper to crunch into the rear of the Sierra. McCarter felt the impact and fought to regain control of his car. At the same time he pushed up his speed again, drawing away from the slowed Mercedes.

The gap between the two cars lessened swiftly as the Mercedes picked up speed again. This time the driver of the Mercedes cut to the third lane, bringing his vehicle alongside McCarter's. A window was powered down and the squat snout of a suppressed Ingram appeared.

"Oh no, you don't," McCarter yelled. He stamped on the Sierra's brake pedal, letting the Mercedes shoot ahead, then before the driver could adjust his speed, McCarter hauled on the wheel of his Ford and rammed the side of the Mercedes.

Metal grated and sparks flew as the two cars, briefly locked together, battled their way along the empty stretch of road.

Regaining control of his vehicle, the Mercedes's driver swung his wheel in an attempt to shove the Sierra away. The German car was the heavier vehicle, and the solid mass of its weight began to affect the Sierra.

Once more McCarter braked, allowing his car to drop right back. He swung the wheel and fell in right behind the Mercedes.

"Now it's my turn, pal," he said with a grin.

He had the Korth Magnum at his side, fully loaded again, and with deliberate intent McCarter rolled down his window. He took the gun in his right hand, steering with his left, and stuck the Magnum out the window. Just at that moment the Mercedes's driver gunned his motor and the car began to pull away, but the diesel engine was a touch slow to respond.

"Just give me one more second," McCarter asked, then steadied himself and opened fire.

He emptied all six chambers into the Mercedes. One shot missed, but the other five struck home. The right rear tire was blown off, and three projectiles ruptured the fuel tank.

McCarter fell way back as the speeding Mercedes began to veer wildly. The burst tire exposed the steel rim of the wheel, which threw up an arc of bright sparks when the spinning wheel struck the surface of the road. Despite the driver's attempts to keep it on a straight course, the Mercedes swerved from left to right, back and forth across the three lanes. On one of its right-hand curves it struck the central guard rail. More sparks flew, mingled with debris. Bouncing on and off the barrier, the Mercedes was suddenly completely out of control. The driver had lost it. He panicked, jerked the wheel and slammed on the brakes. The big, heavy car shuddered, slammed into the barrier again, and then, almost in slow motion, it flipped over and started sliding along on its roof.

McCarter drove on by without a backward glance. He was rid of his pursuers. His priority now was to contact Hal Brognola as soon as he could get back to his hotel.

A vivid flash of light in the rearview mirror made him glance up. The overturned Mercedes had erupted in a boiling mass of flame. The igniting gasoline mushroomed up and out, engulfing the car from end to end in a billowing, blistering wave of fire.

4

It was after 1.30 a.m. when McCarter got back to his hotel—the Holiday Inn. He parked the battered Sierra and made his way to his room, where he immediately picked up the telephone and dialed the special number code that would put him through to Stony Man via the communications satellite link. Fed through some of the most sophisticated security and scrambler systems, the Stony Man headquarters communications setup was as near perfect as possible.

McCarter waited impatiently while Hal Brognola was contacted. He was in the middle of some briefing conference apparently. Who was being briefed? McCarter wondered. Able Team? Phoenix Force itself? Or maybe Brognola was in contact with the big guy—the formerly "outlawed" Mack Bolan. Which had been just a load of bull as far as David McCarter was concerned. Bolan was never more of an outlaw than the rest of them. He'd simply found that he couldn't work within the Stony Man setup after the devastating attack that had breached security and wiped out everything he held dear. Bolan had quit the sanctioned operation and had gone solo for a while, operating the only way he knew how. Exacting justice for those who were helplessly on the receiving end of the savages' fury. The world was in a mess, and Bolan was doing his utmost to redress the balance. As far as McCarter was concerned Bolan was doing fine, and as much as he was able the Briton would back Bolan any time the opportunity arose, though Bolan was once again loosely affiliated with the powers that be.

"David?" Brognola's voice came over the line with some surprise. "Do you have a problem?"

"In a word—yes," McCarter answered.

"Go ahead, I'm listening."

McCarter related everything that had happened from the moment Jake Tasker had shown up in the Dog and Partridge. Brognola listened without interruption until McCarter uttered one particular word. *Manta.*

"Are you absolutely certain it was Manta?"

"Yes, of course I'm certain," McCarter replied testily. "I'm not bloody deaf."

Brognola ignored the sarcasm. "All right, David. Now I want you to do something for me. No questions or protests. Just sit tight. Don't leave your room. Have your meals sent up, watch the TV and wait for Phoenix Force to join you."

"So Manta does mean something to you! I knew it. Come on, Hal, spill the beans," McCarter rattled excitedly.

"Yakov will fill you in," Brognola said in his sternest don't-argue-with-me tone.

"Okay." McCarter relented. "But tell the guys not to take too long. I hate sitting around."

HAL BROGNOLA HAD JUST CUT the connection. He put the phone down and turned back to the Stony Man War Room conference table, around which sat the rest of Phoenix Force. "As usual," he commented, "our delinquent McCarter has already committed himself."

"To what?" asked Gary Manning, the Force's Canadian member.

"Trust David to go somewhere and find a real trouble spot. To the very problem I was about to brief you guys on," the Fed explained with a disbelieving smile on his force.

"That's David," Calvin James said with a grin. "One crazy dude."

"It's the kind of craziness we need," Manning added.

He and McCarter were always hurling throwaway jokes at each other. To an outsider they might have seemed serious, but as far as McCarter and Manning were concerned, it was a way of easing the tension of their often odious missions. Although, admittedly, it was also a method that allowed them to accommodate their very different natures. Their profession meant they were operating under extreme pressure for long periods. One of the ways the Phoenix members had of relieving that pressure was their off-the-wall humor. It was a necessary safety valve.

Gary Manning knew the need for such relief. The Canadian powerhouse thrived on tough assignments. He was one of the world's leading demolition experts and had "graduated" from the Canadian army, where he was also one of the best rifle shots ever, to a tour of duty in Vietnam as an "observer". In truth Manning had been working with the Fifth Special Forces and the Special Observations Group, where his demolition skills had been frequently used in destroying NVA bases. Through his involvement Manning had become one of the few Canadians to win the Silver Star for valor.

After Vietnam the Royal Canadian Mounted Police accepted Manning, and such were his talents that he was assigned to the force's antiterrorist division. When the West German government created their GSG-9 elite antiterrorist group, Manning was sent to work with them under an exchange scheme. He was recalled home when the RCMP wrapped up its intelligence operation and was offered a safe desk job. Manning's refusal was blunt and to the point, and he quit the RCMP and went to work in the private sector of business.

He gave marriage a try. It didn't last and was swiftly dissolved. Manning concentrated on his career. It wasn't long before he was hired by North American International as a high-salary security consultant. This was the position he was holding when he was approached and asked to join the newly created Phoenix Force. The rest had become history.

Despite his snappishness with McCarter at times, Gary Manning would have been the first to stand up for the Briton. McCarter was brash and had an impulsive nature that more often than not simply attracted trouble. He could be, and often was rude—especially in the face of pomposity and authority—and became bored and frustrated during lulls between the action. On the other hand, there was no better man to have at your side in the middle of a firefight. McCarter was a born warrior. He lived for action, and when the chips were down, the odds overwhelming, that was when David McCarter became the driving force behind the team's strike back.

"So what is this all about?" asked Colonel Yakov Katzenelenbogen, Phoenix Force's unit commander. His physical appearance was more like that of a professor than of one of the world's leading crack antiterrorist fighters. Katz had iron-gray hair and mild blue eyes, and even showed the slightest beginnings of a paunch. But he was more than a match for any adversary, even with the loss of his right forearm. That had happened during the Six-Day War. In that conflict Katz had also lost his only son. That loss was one of many he had suffered during his life.

The son of Russian Jews, Katz had been brought up in France after his parents fled there following the Bolshevik Revolution. As a young boy Katz had learned to speak English, Russian, French and German, and those languages had been of great use to him during the Second World War, when he had joined the underground resistance movement. Later his skills were put to good use by the OSS, when the Americans recruited him. Following the war Katz had joined the Haganah in Palestine, fighting for the state of Israel and independence.

Katz's expertise also drew him into Mossad, Israel's major intelligence and espionage organization. It brought him into contact with other agencies—CIA, British SIS, French Sûreté and even the West German BND. Eventually he was contacted and offered command of Phoenix Force, which was part of Mack Bolan's Stony Man organization. Along with Bolan himself, Phoenix Force was the third arm of the Stony Man Triad. Able Team completed the lineup.

Hal Brognola chewed on his unlit cigar thoughtfully. He tapped a manila folder that lay on the table in front of him.

"Three days ago a man named Phillip Harriman was kidnapped from his London home. Harriman, an American citizen, has been working on an ultrasecret project with the British defense ministry. The project, code-named Manta, is a mobile missile system capable of transporting and launching a new generation cruise-type weapon. Manta is a versatile missile, capable of being used as a strike weapon on fixed targets or as a battlefield missile. It has a maximum range of six hundred miles. It can be fitted with a variety of warheads, conventional or nuclear. The word from the White House is that Manta is state-of-the-art missile design and performance. Full marks go to Phillip Harriman for his computer genius. He's designed and programmed the system that launches and tells the missile where to go. In every test Manta has undergone, the failure rate is zero."

"Sounds almost too good to be true," Calvin James remarked. The black Phoenix Force member never took anything at face value. He needed a whole lot of proof before he accepted any given statement.

The youngest Phoenix Force member, James made up for his lack of years with hard, practical experience. Raised on the rough South Side of Chicago, James had joined the Navy at seventeen. His natural skill and dedication eventually brought him to the attention of the SEALs, which resulted in his spending two years with a special-operations group in Vietnam. As fate would have it, James was wounded during his final SOG mission. He returned home with an honorable discharge and a medal.

Shortly after he had commenced his studies in medicine and chemistry at UCLA, his mother and sister both met untimely and unnatural deaths. That prompted him to scrap his planned studies and go in for police science. He later joined the police department of San Francisco, and was eventually recruited into the city's SWAT team. Phoenix Force had approached him—initially during an actual SWAT operation—and James had become a permanent member of the team.

Brognola flashed a delayed smile at James's comment. "Oh, it's true right enough."

"So it's good," Manning said, "and it's ultra-secret. So how come somebody snatched the guy who designed it if it isn't supposed to exist?"

"Obviously somebody knows," James said. "Any idea who?"

"We have candidates now," Brognola told them. "Since David's call."

"Has he found the kidnappers?" Katz asked, lighting his second cigarette since entering the War Room. He asked almost casually, as if McCarter's finding the criminals was just an everyday happening. Which could have been true. David McCarter did have a nose for sniffing out things from the most innocent surroundings. He had an inborn knack for it.

Truly accomplished as a national champion at pistol shooting, David McCarter was also highly skilled with any type of weapon and in any form of combat. He was an excellent pilot, as well. McCarter had served with the British Strategic Air Service. He had seen action all over the world, including Southeast Asia and Oman, and had spent two years undercover while infiltrating Communist cells in Hong Kong. Northern Ireland had also been on the McCarter beat. In 1980 he had been one of the SAS commandos involved in the brilliantly staged raid on the Iranian embassy in London. McCarter thrived on the excitement of his profession. He was also a natural when it came to smelling out trouble, and Katz's statement could easily have been true.

"In a roundabout way I believe he may have done just that," Brognola said. He then repeated his conversation with McCarter for the benefit of the group.

"Are you saying Harriman has been kidnapped because someone may want him to help them gain control of the Manta system?" Katz asked.

"It's a logical assumption," Brognola agreed.

Katz was watching Brognola very closely. "If that is the case, then these people are either very confident they can get their hands on the Manta missiles—or they already have them."

"I had a feeling you'd figure that out pretty fast. The truth is that in the early hours of Tuesday morning—two days ago—the Manta system was hijacked. A combined British-U.S. military team putting the units through some field trials was killed. Four Manta units were taken, and have vanished from Salisbury Plain where the trials were conducted."

"So our terrorists have the weapons, and it sounds like they also have the man who can provide them with access to the launching computers," Katz summed up.

"That's about it," Brognola said. "The only bright thing in this whole damn mess is that the Manta missiles are not fitted with warheads."

"That's just peachy," Calvin James muttered.

"I'll throw in our final piece of information," Brognola said. "We learned a short while ago that Phillip Harriman's wife and his sixteen-year-old daughter are missing. Apparently they were on vacation at their ranch in New Mexico. Now they have vanished."

"Too many pieces to be passed off as coincidence," Rafael Encizo said, speaking for the first time since the briefing had started. "So I'm guessing that vacation time is over for us, too."

Encizo had escaped from his native Cuba to the United States as a youth, after trying to fight back against Castro's Communist soldiers. During the terror that had swept the island after the 1959 revolution, Encizo lost most of his family. His younger brother and two sisters had vanished into a "reeducation" center.

In 1961 Encizo had returned to Cuba in the Bay of Pigs invasion. The abortive attempt to overthrow Castro had been doomed from the start, and many freedom-loving Cubans had died. Encizo himself had been captured and thrown into Castro's infamous El Principe political prison. But he had jumped his wardens, and at the first opportunity Encizo made a break for freedom and returned to the United States.

He had become a naturalized American citizen, working as a diving instructor, bodyguard and treasure hunter. He even did a spell as a maritime insurance investigator. From time to time he took on missions into Central and South America on behalf of law-enforcement agencies. He was wary, though, of trusting their intelligence. The Bay of Pigs fiasco haunted him.

When Phoenix Force came up with an offer for Encizo, he was attracted by the fact that the force would work on its own. They would not have to depend on others too much for backup. Phoenix Force, a band of elite experts, was unique. It would stand or fall by its own hand. Encizo liked that: being in control of his own destiny.

"We going traveling?" James asked.

Brognola nodded. "I'm going to have to split up you guys for this one. Calvin and Rafael, I want you to get out to New Mexico. Mrs. Harriman and her daughter are your concern. If they are being held by the same group of terrorists, it will be so they can be used to force him to cooperate. We have to get them back unharmed, if possible.

"Yakov, you and Gary will be flying to England. Join up with David and find the people who have Harriman and the Mantas."

"We're going to be a little undermanned over there," Manning pointed out."

"Arrangements are under way to fly Karl Hahn over to England to help out. He'll meet you there."

Katz nodded. "That's fine. By the way, how do we play this with the British authorities?"

"The President has cleared everything with the British prime minister. You'll be given a free hand to conduct your investigations in the manner you see fit. A government official will liaise with you and provide whatever you need. He will meet you at your arrival point and take you to a safehouse in London that will serve as your headquarters. A secure line will be available at all times so we can talk directly."

"What is our priority?" Katz inquired.

"Ideally, the safe return of the Mantas and Phillip Harriman. If you can't get either back, the only consideration would be for termination and destruction."

"Kill Harriman and blow up the missiles?" Manning repeated. "I don't mind blitzing machinery—but

I'm not happy about blowing away a guy just because
I can't take him home.''

"Do you think I enjoy giving you orders like that,
Gary? Hell, we're not assassins,'' Brognola snapped.
"But there are times you play all the cards and all there
is left is the wild one. When you play the game, you
might not like the hand you've been dealt. But at least
you have the option of stopping the other guy coming
out a winner.''

"I guess so,'' Manning agreed reluctantly. "Just
remind me never to play poker with you, Hal.''

"One point we haven't covered,'' Katz said. "Are
we assuming that if these RBP characters have the
Mantas *and* Harriman they intend to use the missiles?''

"It is one conclusion,'' Brognola agreed. "Not the
only conclusion but one we have to accept as possible.''

"All right,'' Katz went on. "If the intention is to use
the missiles, we need to add two more factors. One—
the terrorists will need warheads. Two—what are their
targets?''

"Does it have to be 'targets'?'' James asked.
"Couldn't it be a single objective?''

Manning leaned forward. "No, I think Katz has a
point. If you only have a single target you only need
one missile. One mobile unit is trouble enough trun-
dling around the countryside. Why hijack four of the
damn things unless you need them?''

"Let's assume the worst,'' said Brognola. "That
there are four possible target sites. And that the terrorists need four nuclear warheads.''

"Those things aren't just lying around," Encizo exclaimed. "On the other hand, everything can be bought for the right price these days."

"Or stolen," James suggested. "Remember that nuclear device stolen for the Nuclear Free Australia group?" He was referring to a one-kiloton "backpack bomb" stolen in the United States and transported to Australia where it was to have been detonated at the Sydney Opera House. The explosion would have devastated the city—except it never happened because Phoenix Force was involved and removed the threat of nuclear hell in a rain of bullets.

"The options are all open," Brognola admitted. "I'll have our computers do some checking, give us any rundowns on possible thefts. Anything we can tie in to what we already know. I'll do the same on likely targets. It may help."

Katz nodded. "If that's all, Hal, we'd better get organized."

"Your transport will be ready when you are." Brognola stood, unconsciously peeling the wrapper off a fresh cigar. "Good luck, fellers," he added.

Encizo smiled without humor. "We're going to need something closer to a miracle to pull this one all together."

5

As the door of his cell opened, Phillip Harriman sat bolt upright on the hard chair, his heart pounding and his stomach churning.

Harriman didn't consider himself a coward, but he was ready to admit to being scared. The main contributor to his fear was simple ignorance. He had been in the hands of his kidnappers for approximately three days, and up to now they had not given him any indication why they had kidnapped him. Being left in the dark as to the reason was worse than the physical discomforts he was having to endure. Not that they were all that extreme. He was being fed, allowed to drink and was even escorted to the toilet at intervals. Apart from that he was left entirely alone in a bleak, dimly lit room that contained nothing more than a chair and a bed.

The solitude allowed Harriman ample time for thought. He had devoted long hours attempting to figure out what his kidnappers wanted. He did possess knowledge that an enemy might have use for. His involvement in defense work could invite unwanted attention from certain quarters, though the possibility of its actually occurring had never really ingrained itself on Harriman's mind. There was also the chance that he had been kidnapped for purely financial motives. Harriman was not a poor man. He earned good money from his work, and he also had a substantial private income from sources left to him by his late father. Whatever the reason was for his kidnapping, Harriman had not been informed and no demands had been made on him. He wanted to know, needed to know, mainly for his peace of mind. Not knowing added to the feeling of menace that surrounded him.

He didn't even know where he was. From the moment he'd been grabbed and bundled into the back of the panel truck that had pulled up beside him in the street, he'd been kept in isolation. In the truck a cloth hood had been placed over his head, plunging him into total darkness. After what had seemed an endless journey the truck had stopped. Harriman had been pulled from the vehicle and manhandled into a building, up some stairs and into a room. Then the hood had been removed, and Harriman was left alone and friendless in the room that had become his world and his prison cell.

He watched the door open. Three men entered. They were dressed in ordinary everyday clothing with nothing to make any of them stand out in a crowd. The last man to enter closed the door and stood with his back to it. He held a stubby SMG in his hands.

Harriman recognized one of the other men as the one who brought him his food and water, a tall, cold-eyed individual who always seemed to have a faint smile playing around the corners of his wide mouth. He was, Harriman had decided earlier, the kind of man you mistrusted on sight. Beside him stood a shorter, broad-shouldered man. His head was set atop a short, thick neck, and his skull was totally devoid of hair. In contrast his bushy black brows bristled over small, very black glittering eyes that seemed to bore deep into Harriman's very soul.

"So, Phillip, you have had ample time to yourself," the bald man said. His English was good but held a trace of an accent Harriman could not identify. "Are you ready for some conversation now?"

"Depends on the subject," Harriman replied, determined not to let the man dominate him.

"I think we all know why we are here, Phillip."

"The hell we do," Harriman snapped; he was ready for an argument. "Where am I and what am I doing here?"

"Where you are doesn't matter. The reason why is simple. You have skills we need. Skills you will utilize for us. Your scientific expertise."

"No way!" Harriman shook his head. "You just go to hell."

"We appear to have a communication problem, Phillip," the bald man said lightly. He indicated his tall, silent companion. "This is Judson. He is very experienced when it comes to dealing with communication problems. Show Phillip."

Judson faced Harriman. He reached out with a large hand and took hold of Harriman's shirtfront, pulling him to his feet.

"Go ahead," urged the bald man.

Judson's smile flickered, then he punched Harriman in the stomach. Very hard and very low. He did the same thing again and again. The pain was excruciating and so intense that the shock of it made Harriman cry out. Tears burst from his eyes. He would have slumped to the floor if Judson had not retained his grip on Harriman's shirt. Harriman felt sick. His body was aflame. Pain radiated out from the place in his stomach where Judson had been hitting him. He was oblivious to Judson's next move. When Judson's fist crashed against the side of his face, the force of the powerful impact rocked his head back. Again the blow was repeated, slapping Harriman's head back and forth. When he delivered the final blow, Judson released his hold on Harriman's shirt.

Harriman was flung back across the room. He lost his balance and fell to the floor where he lay in a spreading pool of his own blood. He found out later that he had bitten his tongue. The brassy taste of blood filled his mouth and blocked his nose. Some ran down his throat, making him gasp for air. He lay still, not daring to move. His body was racked with pain. His face felt swollen and parts of it seemed to have gone numb. Even though he lay motionless the floor seemed to be tilting beneath him. He could barely think because his senses had been so savagely disturbed.

Dimly he heard the voice of the bald man again. It seemed to come from a long way away, but it was very clear.

"Take a little more time to consider your response, Phillip. I will talk to you again in two hours. Mr. Judson will look forward with interest to your answer."

They left him lying on the floor. It took him almost half an hour to drag himself to the bed. He hauled his pain-racked body onto the dirty mattress, where he lay as still as he could. Harriman had never experienced such pain. That was because he had never been physically beaten before. When he reflected on it, he saw that the whole of his life had been conducted in well-ordered comfort, far removed from the baser side of civilization. Even his work, though devoted to the creation of machines capable of dealing out mass destruction, took place in secure, regulated places where the only intrusive noise came from the air-conditioning units. Harriman knew good living, fine wine and food, enjoyed Bach and Brubeck. He possessed a keen, mathematically inclined mind that had taken him to the peak of his profession, and as yet he had barely tapped the rich vein of his brain's potential.

Right now all that intellectual acumen was of no earthly use to Phillip Harriman. He was faced by uncompromising people who used violence and terror as the tools of their trade. And Harriman, determined though he was not to fall in with their wishes, was not entirely certain he would be able to resist them permanently.

6

Faint noises encroached on David McCarter's sleep-drugged senses. He forced open one eye. Sunlight gleamed behind the drawn curtains, and from its strength McCarter guessed it was midmorning. Before turning in, he had told the night clerk on the desk that he did not want to be disturbed until at least midday. The sounds he could hear told him that someone was in his room, so unless room service had ignored his request for privacy—in which case someone was going to get into trouble—his visitor, or visitors, were intruders and therefore unwelcome.

McCarter held himself motionless, gathering his strength for what was about to come. Whoever was in his room, they weren't there to sell him Girl Guide cookies. Anyone low enough to creep around the way these buggers were just had to be trouble, McCarter decided. He also had a fair idea who his visitors were. If he was right he was in for a hectic time. At that thought his spirits rose considerably. Just anticipating the possibility of action cheered the Cockney hell-raiser no end. He could obey Brognola's order to stay put in his room and still get some exercise. This really was room service.

He concluded that his visitors had to be from the group he'd tangled with earlier. As far as McCarter knew, he hadn't upset anyone else since arriving in England. But he had inflicted damage on the RBP. They would be looking for him without a doubt. McCarter had been associated with Jake Tasker and that would be enough to generate interest in him. The RBP would need to know how much information, if any, Tasker had given him. And they wouldn't be forgetting the RBP members McCarter had canceled out.

McCarter didn't know how many intruders were in his room, or whether they were armed. Only one way to find out he decided.

His eyes snapped wide open, searching. He saw a heavy-set man dressed in nondescript clothing moving in on the bed. The guy wasn't armed, but he had large hands with scarred knuckles. A street tough sent along to do the dirty work. McCarter knew that the brawler wouldn't be on his own. He was there to provide muscle. There would be someone else—out of McCarter's sight—directing things. Maybe more than one. McCarter gave an inward sigh. What the hell! He couldn't lie in bed all day figuring the odds. Not with his bruiser friend closing in. It was time to grab some advantage, even if it was a bad situation.

McCarter moved instinctively, kicking aside the covers and rolling off the bed. As he landed on hands and knees, he lashed out with his left leg, driving the heel of his foot into the bruiser's groin. The tough guy let out a howl of agony as McCarter's crippling blow disabled him. Continuing his move, McCarter arched away from the bed, aware of the rush of sound from the far side of the room. He half rose to his feet, sensing the closeness of the injured tough, and slammed his elbow into the man's soft gut. Rancid breath exploded from the guy's mouth. A microsecond later

McCarter had risen to his full height, still turning, bringing the heel of his palm around to connect with the intruder's nose. McCarter heard the satisfying crunch of shattered cartilage and saw the guy's face blossom red. Then he chopped a hard-edged palm to the stunned guy's neck, driving him to the floor.

Even as the street brawler was falling, McCarter had pivoted on his heels to face the rest of the visitors.

There were two of them.

One was another street punk, though younger than the first, with short blond hair and a sallow face. He was grinning the insane grin of the manic psychopath—a degenerate with little regard for human life or dignity, who enjoyed inflicting and witnessing violence. There were a lot of them around at the present time, McCarter knew. Too many. They reveled in horror and destruction, having no purpose or ambition other than to inflict pain and suffering on others. They were the types who orchestrated soccer violence, bringing the game into disrepute with their brutality to the loyal, decent fans of the game. It was this kind of scum who attacked the innocent without warning or provocation, committing senseless acts of degrading violence for no other reason than the kick they got from it. Mindless savagery seemed to be the order of the day. It was becoming all too familiar, a frightening malady of the age.

These antisocial misfits, McCarter reasoned, were just the kind of recruits the RBP would be seeking. Give them a collective urge to destroy, to smash and maim, in the name of the party that would eliminate the ruling class, and these vicious men would flock to join. It was so easy to inflame the smoldering violence lurking in the hearts of these lost souls and to fill their festering minds with ideological claptrap so they would explode on an unsuspecting world and flood it with their scorching rebellion. There were always those who were ready to use such pliable personalities for achieving their own ends. But that wasn't anything new. The ambition of evil had fed from the fire of mass hysteria before.

Having taken account of the young punk, McCarter flicked his gaze beyond to somebody standing farther back. Though in outward appearance the man was similar to the others, McCarter registered a subtle difference in the man's bearing. This one was a leader, not a minion. He directed the action. Probably he was quite capable of inflicting violence on others himself, but it would be done dispassionately and calmly, with cold deliberation. There was no empty mind here. No urban savage waiting to be turned into a zombie. This man resorted to thought, and manipulated the vacant minds. And that made him potentially a greater threat.

The first street tough was going down, and McCarter had already turned toward the blond punk, seeing him rush around the end of the bed, eager to prove himself. He proved only that he was no expert in combat as he lunged wildly at McCarter. The Phoenix warrior leaned away from the uncoordinated attack. As the punk was carried forward and down by his own momentum, McCarter drove his right knee into the man's body and heard the sound of ribs cracking. The punk collapsed to his knees, hunched over, moaning softly.

McCarter had been expecting to hear the oiled sound of a gun being cocked. Even so it pulled him up hard, and he glared at the third man and his leveled weapon.

"That's not playing by the rules," McCarter protested.

The gunman allowed himself a thin smile. "There are no rules. Now get some clothes on and let's all get out of here." He spoke with an American accent, and the way he handled himself identified the man to McCarter as military or ex-military.

McCarter, turning to the chair where his street clothes lay, suddenly remembered he was stark naked, having leaped straight out of bed.

"Too much to expect you to close your eyes, I suppose?" he asked the gunman, who responded by waggling the barrel of his gun. "Pervert," McCarter muttered under his breath as he started to dress.

A short time later McCarter was being escorted down to the hotel fire stairs to the basement car park. There was a car waiting in one of the vacant parking lots. It was a large 2.5 Rover. McCarter was told to get in the back seat and the gun-wielding American joined him. The blond punk, still clutching his damaged ribs, slouched behind the wheel, while his partner slumped drunkenly beside him. His white face was caked in dried blood from his crushed nose.

"No heroics," the American warned.

McCarter grinned. "You talking to me or them?"

"A real smartass. Listen, pal, my orders are to bring you in alive, but don't think I wouldn't kill you if it needed doing."

McCarter kept his mouth shut. There were times when silence was the safest route, and this was one of them.

The American produced a black hood from his pocket. He handed it to McCarter. The Briton pulled the garment over his head, sitting back in complete darkness. He should have expected that. His captors wouldn't want him to know their destination.

He heard the car start, felt it roll forward. At the exit the Rover turned left. McCarter concentrated on the route, trying to get a clue as to what direction they were traveling. After a quarter of an hour he deduced that his captors had anticipated him. The Rover was making endless turns, both right and left, leaving him confused as to which way they were going.

Beside McCarter the American leaned forward. "All right," he said. "Head for base now."

Under the hood McCarter grinned. Score one for the bad guys. They'd outthought him on this one. McCarter didn't worry too much. The game was far from over, and he would get a turn yet.

7

A charter plane flew Rafael Encizo and Calvin James to New Mexico, where it landed at the small airfield that served the town of Trinity. The ranch owned by Phillip Harriman lay some miles beyond the town. The two Phoenix Force warriors dumped their luggage in the Chrysler 4 × 4 waiting for them and drove the eight miles to Trinity. They arrived in town on the stroke of noon.

Trinity lay baking beneath the hot New Mexico sun, and as he drove along the main street, Calvin James felt as though he'd seen the place before. He finally recognized that Trinity looked like a Western movie set with its dusty street and sun-bleached adobe buildings. There were even a few horses standing listlessly at hitch rails, heads down and tails twitching to shoo away the clouds of offending flies. James half expected to see John Wayne come lumbering out of the saloon as he drove by, and he couldn't hold back a self-conscious smile.

"It's a different world," Encizo said, "out here away from the city."

"Yeah, if you like it quiet," James added.

Toward the far end of town he spotted the sheriff's office. It was a stone building, with a tall flagpole rising from a circular concrete base fronting it. There were a couple of patrol cars parked outside, the insignia of the Trinity County Sheriff emblazoned on the front doors.

James parked the Chrysler in a slot reserved for visitors, then he and Encizo climbed out. The fierce heat of the day hit them as they exited the 4 × 4's air-conditioned cab.

"That is *hot!*" James commented as they made their way to the main building.

It was cooler inside. And quiet. All they could hear was the subdued hum of the building's air conditioner and the distant ring of a telephone. The reception area had a tiled floor and was decorated with Indian artifacts and old photographs of Trinity during its pioneer days. There was a wide reception desk, behind which sat a beautiful black-haired Indian girl, wearing the uniform of the sheriff's department.

"May I help you?" she asked.

James nodded. "We'd like to see Sheriff Costigan. He is expecting us. Mr. Black and Mr. Brown." He used their cover names for this assignment.

The girl frowned slightly, then recovered her composure and smiled again. She picked up a phone. "If you would like to take a seat, I'll see if Sheriff Costigan is free."

James and Encizo settled into comfortable leather chairs as the girl spoke to someone over the phone. After a short time she replaced the phone and turned toward them. "Sheriff Costigan will be with you shortly."

Costigan was six-six and broad shouldered. He wore a tan uniform and pants and brown Western-style boots. His blue eyes made a vivid contrast with his sun-browned face and dark hair. He thrust out a large, powerful hand in welcome.

"Step inside, fellers," he said. His deep voice delivered the words almost lazily. Costigan might have sounded a trifle slow, but Encizo and James were aware they were dealing with a professional lawman. The man was nobody's fool.

They stepped into the office he indicated, and James performed the brief introduction. They were in a spacious, uncluttered room, light and airy. A large picture window behind the sheriff's desk offered an unobstructed panorama of the sweeping New Mexico landscape. In the distance a hazy line of hills marked the horizon.

When they were all seated, with Costigan facing the Phoenix men over his wide desk, the sheriff broke the silence. "I had the nod you boys were on your way. Talked to a high-up from the Justice Department who asked me to cooperate and give you fellers a free hand. So fire away."

"We are grateful for your help, Sheriff," Encizo said.

"The bottom line seems to be that this Harriman kidnap is government business and I have to stand back," Costigan said, showing that he fully understood Washington's request. He watched Encizo and James for a reaction.

"That's what the circumstances call for, Sheriff. All we ask is that you give us whatever information you have, then let us go on our way," Calvin James explained, trying to make it easy on Costigan. It was not always pleasant having to walk in on the local law to tell them to step aside and not interfere.

"Sure," Costigan said without malice. He stood up and crossed the room to a bubbling percolator. "Coffee?"

"Yes," James said. "Thanks."

"Black for me," Encizo added.

"What do you have on the kidnap?" James asked.

Costigan began pouring coffee into thick mugs. "We received the call midmorning the day the Harrimans vanished. Mailman phoned from the house to say he'd found the place deserted, with signs of a struggle having taken place. I drove out there—it's a horse ranch about sixteen miles up the road—and found the house wide open. Car in the yard with the keys in the ignition. Some broken pots in the kitchen. Radio still on. Nothing taken, so it wasn't robbery. Me and my deputy went right through the place. The only missing things were Julie—Mrs. Harriman—and Lucy, her daughter."

After Costigan handed out the steaming mugs, he folded his tall frame behind the desk again.

"No other people about the ranch to see anything?" Encizo asked.

Costigan shook his head. "The Harrimans' crew—just two hands—are up the hills somewhere on a horse hunt. Been gone a couple of days."

"Any tracks to follow?" asked James.

"Some, but they just led back to the highway, and we lost them there."

Encizo understood that Costigan had finished. "That it?"

Costigan smiled. "Yeah. Sorry, fellers, but that was all she wrote."

James swallowed some coffee, then swirled some around in his mug. He shot a keen glance at the sheriff. "Okay, we have the facts. Now what about the theories?"

"You mean, do I have any?"

"Yes. This is your territory. We don't know it from a hole in the ground. Frankly, we need your help to start moving in the right direction."

Costigan thought for a few seconds. "Look, I know you can't tell me what this kidnapping means, but I can make an educated guess. It has to be more than a couple of dopeheads snatching somebody for a handful of dollar bills. The way Washington put the hammer down and sent you boys to take over—well, we got to have something pretty high-powered here." He eyed the Phoenix men suggestively. "At least tell me I'm inside the ballpark."

"You're in," James admitted, prepared to allow Costigan a glimmer of light to illuminate the darkness he was groping around in.

"Fine," Costigan said. "So we can safely figure we're dealing with out-of-towners. Hell, we ain't got any local criminals smart enough to pull a deal like this. It helps. I can put out the word for information on any strangers in the area."

"We don't know how many were involved," Encizo pointed out.

"At the end of the day I might even be able to tell you that, Mr. Brown," Costigan informed him with a grin.

"Your local eyes and ears that good?" James asked.

"Hell, yes," Costigan said. "This might be big country but it gets pretty damn tight when it comes to strange faces showing up. Out of state accents get noticed, or somebody asking questions."

"What about hotels? Motels?" Encizo suggested. "Our people would need a base while they got things set up."

"There's a motel on the edge of town. Nearest after that would be the Desert Halt about thirty miles west."

"Could be a likely spot," James said. "I'd expect them to use something away from town."

Encizo nodded. "We'll check it out. And take a look at the Harriman place."

Costigan got up and crossed to a large map pinned to the wall. He showed the Phoenix pair the locations of the motel and the Harriman ranch. "Ask for Sam Hild at the motel. He owns the place and runs it. Tell him I said to help all he can. Meantime I'll get my boys to do some checking on any newcomers in the area."

They finished their coffee, then Encizo and James said their goodbyes to Costigan and left the building, returning to the 4×4. James started the motor and pulled away from the parking area, back onto the street. He turned the Chrysler west and drove out of Trinity.

They made the trip in silence. Forty minutes hadn't quite passed when James was pulling the Chrysler off the highway and rolling to a stop before the Desert Halt motel office.

There was a deserted look to the motel, which consisted of a line of weathered wooden cabins joined together by a covered walkway. The place hadn't had a lick of paint in years. A single vehicle was parked halfway along the row of cabins.

"Hey," James remarked as they climbed out of the Chrysler, "do you think Norman Bates works here?"

Encizo glanced at his partner, shaking his head at James's remark.

Inside the motel office a balding man with a sagging beer belly was leafing through the newspaper he had spread out on the desk. When Encizo and James stepped into the stuffy room, he glanced up questioningly.

"Mr. Hild?" Encizo asked.

"Yeah," the man said. "Can I help you?"

Encizo flashed the Justice Department badge he and the other Phoenix Force members carried in order to authenticate their cover identities. "My partner and I are conducting an investigation. We've just come from a meeting with Sheriff Costigan in Trinity. He feels you may be able to help us, Mr. Hild."

Hild relaxed when he realized he was assisting in an investigation. "What can I tell you?"

"Have you had any out-of-state guests within the past week? Maybe a small group? Four, maybe five men? Take your time."

"Don't have to," Hild said. "There was a group. Six guys. City types. I figured they was from back east somewhere. They booked in five days back. Stayed for three days, then paid up one morning and took off."

"You recall anything about them?" asked James.

"Not a great deal. I don't pay much attention. Anyhow, they didn't show their faces much. Apart from when they went out for food. There's a diner about five miles farther west. They'd send one guy out, and he'd come back with stuff."

"They say what they were doing out here?"

"Property developers," Hild told Encizo, apparently eager to answer any question. "I reckon that was a heap of shit. But what the hell, they didn't cause any problems. I had no reason to poke my nose in. Man can get his ass blown off askin' too many questions these days. Know what I mean?''

James smiled. "I know what you mean, Mr. Hild."

"What kind of car did they have?" Encizo asked.

"Last year's Buick. Painted black with tinted windows. Can't tell you the number 'cause the plates were always dusty."

"If you see either the car of any of the men, Mr. Hild, we would appreciate a call through Sheriff Costigan's office."

"Sure," Hild said. "My information any good?"

"Very helpful," James said. "Thanks for your cooperation."

"Any time," Hild called as the Phoenix pair returned to their 4 × 4 and drove off.

"What do you think?" James asked as he pushed the Chrysler in the direction of the Harriman ranch turnoff.

"Sounded promising," Encizo said. "All we have to do now is figure out where those guys are hiding out with their hostages."

James grinned. "Ah!" he said. "The easy part of the puzzle." His partner had fallen silent, and James glanced across at him. "You okay, buddy?"

Encizo gave a sigh. "I hate having to say this because it sounds so corny—but I think we're being followed."

"You love saying it," James replied, glancing in the rearview mirror. "And hell, you are right."

"You want to know something else?" Encizo added. "That car. It's a black Buick with tinted windows. Last year's model."

"Huh?" James said. "You sure?"

8

Encizo had reached into the back of the Chrysler for a long carryall lying on the rear seat. He began to unzip it.

Calvin James smiled dryly as out the corner of his eye he watched Encizo pull a Heckler & Koch MP-5 out of the bag.

"Yeah," he said, "I guess you are sure."

Encizo inserted a thirty-round magazine into the MP-5. Then he placed the weapon on the seat beside him and reached inside the holdall again to lift out James's M-16. He also withdrew a magazine of thirty 5.56 mm rounds, which he inserted in the loading slot. Both Phoenix men were already carrying handguns. James had a Colt Commander in a shoulder rig and also had a G-96 dagger attached to the harness under his right arm. Encizo preferred a Cold Steel Tanto knife, fitted with a rubberized handle that gave the user maximum grip and feel of the weapon. His handgun was a Smith & Wesson 9 mm Model 59 with a fourteen-round magazine.

"The turnoff for the Harriman place is about six miles farther on," Encizo said. "Let's see if our friends back there follow. If they do, we'll call their bluff. No chance of any civilians getting hurt once we get on that cross-country dirt road."

James gunned the Chrysler, and the powerful 4×4 ate the empty miles of blacktop with a muted roar. He took a quick look in the rearview mirror and saw that the Buick was keeping up with them.

"Keep right on coming, brother," James murmured. "There may just be a nice surprise waiting for you."

In a short while Encizo tapped James on the arm. "Coming up," he said.

James saw the dusty, unpaved track that led away from the main road to cut its way through the New Mexico landscape. He slowed the Chrysler and swung off the highway. The 4×4 rocked along the undulating trail. On either side lay sun-bleached, sandy terrain. There was little vegetation. Some dusty scrub. Parched clumps of pale grass. The occasional spiky yucca plant.

"He still with us?" James asked after ten minutes of steady driving.

"Hard to tell with all the dust we're kicking up," Encizo said. "It's a good thing we're not trying to hide from the Apaches."

"You said it. Hey, I see him!" James exclaimed as he caught a glimpse of the Buick through the swirling dust. "Persistent bastard, isn't he."

They crested a rise in the trail. Ahead the rutted track curved off to the right, around the base of an eroded outcropping of rock that towered some thirty feet.

"That'll do it," James said, indicating the outcrop. "I'll hit the brakes as soon as we get around that bend. We can take cover on each side of the trail."

Encizo nodded. He pulled out his Model 59 and checked it, then thrust it back into the holster. Then he took a couple of spare magazines from the carryall—one for his MP-5 and one for James's M-16. He dropped one in his jacket and reached over to slip the other into his partner's pocket.

"You set?" James asked and Encizo nodded, picking up his MP-5.

The curve came up on them and James gave the Chrysler plenty of gas, making them go around the base of the high rock swiftly, out of sight of the Buick. As soon as he had completed the turn, he hit the brake, cutting the engine at the same time. The 4×4 slithered to a halt sideways across the trail. Thick dust billowed up around the vehicle.

Encizo already had his door unlatched. He booted it open and jumped, the momentum propelling him away from the vehicle and into the tangled scrub at the side of the track.

Snatching up his M-16, James followed the same procedure. His foot caught against the exposed root of some scrub growing at the edge of the track but he quickly regained his balance and dashed into the brush.

Just then the shadowing Buick broke into view around the curve. Seeing the Chrysler motionless, blocking the track, its doors wide open, the Buick's driver stepped on his brake. The big car plunged to a rocking halt, only inches from the rear of the 4×4. Aware that he had left himself and his companions open to attack, the driver of the Buick quickly put the car into reverse and stepped on the gas. With a howl of protest from its tortured transmission the Buick shot backward. The driver, forgetting he had just negotiated a bend, took the car in a straight line, over the edge of the track and into soft sand piled up there.

Within seconds the whirling wheels at the rear had dug twin trenches, and the heavy Buick simply bottomed out, well and truly stuck.

There were four people in the Buick—including the driver—and the moment they realized what had happened they decided to exit the stranded car. The doors flew open, and the occupants came out low and fast, with automatic weapons on full burn.

The comparative silence of the desert land was suddenly punctuated by the vicious crackle of gunfire, which was directed at the parked Chrysler. The bodywork was punched by concentrated fire. Windows exploded, spraying the 4×4's interior with glittering fragments. Upholstery was ripped apart and the fascia panel shattered in a shower of plastic and disintegrating instruments. As the tires were shredded by the fierce volleys, ragged lumps of rubber flew into the air, and the Chrysler sank onto its wheel rims.

With the rattle of the shots still ringing in the heat-shimmered air, the four gunmen broke ranks, spreading out before they launched a further attack. Encizo, from his concealment to the right of the bullet-scarred 4×4, spotted one of the gunmen moving in his general direction. He eased forward, clearing the yucca blocking his way, and raised his MP-5. The gunman saw Encizo a second too late. He jerked the muzzle of his Uzi around, touching the trigger a fraction prematurely. A stream of hot 9 mms chewed through the scrub.

Then Encizo fired, and his sustained burst caught the man in the abdomen before stitching a ragged line up his torso. The dying gunman was tossed off his feet to flop back over a yucca plant, his head back, his eyes staring up sightlessly into the blazing orb of the sun.

Encizo's volley signaled a flurry of activity from the opposition. They began to move forward, separating as they skirted the bullet-riddled Chrysler. Each man took a different direction and fired as he advanced. Bullets zipped through the scrub, chewing at the vegetation and kicking up geysers of sand.

Some of the blistering shots came uncomfortably close to Calvin James. The black Phoenix warrior found their proximity discomforting, even though the near misses were there more by luck than actual firing skill. He vacated his position fast, twisting his supple body in a low dive that took him away from the hail of death. Landing on his left shoulder, James rolled and came to a rest on his stomach. He thrust his M-16 forward and triggered 3-round bursts at the gunman closest to his position. The guy went down hard as the 5.56 sizzlers chewed his lower legs all the way to the bone. Blood began to surge from the ruined flesh. He landed on his face, choking on the sand that filled his mouth. The impact of his fall jarred the SMG from his hands, leaving him unarmed. Despite his severe wounds he went for the handgun holstered under his jacket. James, still belly down on the ground, altered the angle of the M-16's muzzle and gave the hardman a last burst of 5.56 death dealers. That terminated the exchange between James and his opponent.

Unaware that they had lost one more of their number, the remaining pair of gunmen kept on coming. They were dressed in cheap-looking suits and seemed to be out of their depth in this wild, sun-scorched country. The towering man-made canyons of the urban jungle were more likely their territory. Dark alleys and noisy streets, not the primitive wilderness where combat became a one-to-one encounter and being street wise wasn't enough savvy to survive on.

Rafael Encizo and Calvin James were past masters in the art of jungle and desert combat. They had learned through practical experience, over many missions, that the only way to survive was to become part of the terrain. To use the land and not allow *it* to use them. Previous assignments had seen Phoenix Force blitzing through hostile terrain from South Africa to Thailand to Columbia—all different, all alien environments, yet Phoenix Force had survived each encounter by stealth and skill and because they were the best in their chosen profession.

Now, while the enemy blundered about, heavy-footed, uncertain and very conspicuous, the Phoenix pros melted into the landscape, seeming to vanish into thin air.

"Where'd they go?" one of the gunmen yelled to his partner.

"Hell, I don't know!"

The first gunman paused to jam a fresh clip into his Uzi. That done, he moved on, eyes searching the scrub and grass.

"Hey, Chuck," he suddenly called.

"Yeah?"

"They got Artie... blew his head wide open!"

The one called Chuck swore silently. The job was turning into a damn circus. Two of his guys already wiped out, and now the damn targets had disappeared. He was beginning to wish he had never accepted this contract, never mind that the money was really good. He should have stayed in New York. But he was in the business, and if you put up your shingle saying you took contracts, then you stuck to your word. A deal was a deal.

When he'd taken the contract, it had seemed easy enough. Get a team together and carry out a snatch in New Mexico. Take the merchandise to a holding house and wait to be contacted. Everything had gone according to plan, up until the moment the two men had arrived in town, spending time with the local law before driving out to the Desert Halt motel. Something about the way the newcomers acted had planted the suspicion in Chuck's mind that they might be the law—or even higher. He had figured that he had covered his tracks, but there was always a need for insurance. The people who had hired Chuck and his team had made it clear there were to be no slipups. The kidnap victims had to be kept secure until Chuck received his final instructions.

Mistakes will not be tolerated! That had been the message from the guy who had negotiated the contract. Nothing more was said. There was no need. The warning came through loud and clear. Hold up your end of the deal, or you become expendable. Dead meat.

It was the prime motivation behind Chuck's deciding to keep an eye on arrivals in Trinity and anyone who showed an interest in the motel and the Harriman ranch. Chuck needed to be one step ahead. He had to keep the hostages secure until the safe period was over and the Harriman woman and her daughter outlived their usefulness. After that he was to terminate them.

So Chuck and part of his team had kept watch. Nothing seemed to be happening just as his employer had said. There would, Chuck had been informed, be a clamp on any local law investigating the kidnapping. Even so, Chuck had decided to initiate his own security backup. And he had been rewarded by the appearance of the black guy and his partner. When the pair had left Trinity, Chuck had followed—all the way to the Desert Halt and then in the direction of the Harriman ranch.

And that had done it for Chuck. This pair, he had decided, needed taking out before they got lucky.

Trouble was it hadn't worked out that way. And Chuck was down fifty percent of his team.

He ejected the spent clip from his Uzi and tossed it aside. Fishing a fresh one from his pocket, he jammed it into the slot, banging it home. He slid the cocking button back, chambering the first 9 mm parabellum.

"All right, you bastards," he muttered. "Let's get this mess cleared up."

He caught his man's eye and gave him a look that said he really meant business.

"We'll split, Rick. You go out that way. I'll cut over here. Catch these suckers between us."

Rick nodded and slipped out of sight.

Chuck moved off at an angle, the Uzi ready in his hands. He felt annoyed because of the unexpectedly strong opposition but transferred his annoyance to his surroundings. The problem with this country was the damn silence. There was no sound to cover any noise he might make. He could even hear his own breathing and the gritty crunch of his shoes against the sandy ground. Even the dry rustling of the scrub and grass.

Chuck paused, squatting in the shade of a large spiked yucca plant. Sweat stung his eyes and made his clothes stick to his flesh. He wiped his damp hands down the legs of his pants. He had never known such heat. It was different from the damp, muggy heat of the city. This heat made a man sweat all the time, then sucked up that sweat, drying it instantly. It drained him of moisture and energy. The constant glare of the high, bright sun hurt his eyes, too.

Somewhere—he couldn't quite place the source—he heard a rustling. It might have been a man's clothing snagging against the scrub. Then, it could have been made by an animal passing by.

Chuck hefted the Uzi, deciding it was time to move. He'd had enough pussyfooting around. He didn't give a damn who these hotshots were. They couldn't burn two of his boys and get away with it. He had a reputation to maintain.

He crept forward, parting the coarse grass with the tip of the Uzi. He was certain he had caught movement up ahead. It had to be one of the bastards from the Chrysler. It couldn't be Rick, because he had gone way over the other side of the area. Chuck grinned as he became aware of a fleeting movement again. Of course. It *was* one of them.

The black dude!

Now where had he gone?

The son of a bitch was everywhere.

In his anger Chuck allowed his concentration to slip. He stood upright in an attempt to pinpoint his target again. It proved to be his final mistake.

Calvin James had already pinpointed *his* target. He had seen Chuck in the brief seconds before the man rose to his full height. It was a reckless, careless move, and it was an opportunity James could not afford to pass up. The Phoenix pro almost felt sorry for the guy, but in a combat situation there was little room for sympathy, especially for an enemy who was out to kill you. In a tight situation emotions couldn't be allowed or the result would be to end up like a sieve. Calvin James had been in enough kill-or-be-killed situations to have learned the way the game had to be played: hard, fast and with a degree of ruthless determination to emerge the winner.

He rose out of the desert grass, coming to rest on one knee, his M-16 tracking his target in a smooth curve. Then his finger eased the trigger back. The M-16 spit its trio of death messengers.

The 5.56 projectiles smashed into Chuck's chest, cleaving their way into the heart and destroying it in a microsecond of numbing pain. Moments later he coughed harshly, blood erupting from his mouth as he tumbled awkwardly to the ground, his unfired Uzi spinning from his limp hands.

James sensed movement on the periphery of his vision. He twisted his body around, his M-16 following, ready for another target, and saw the remaining gunman racing toward him. The man was yelling, but it was impossible to hear what he was saying due to the fact that he was firing his Uzi as he ran, making the bullets go wide.

Calvin James held his M-16 steady on the bounding figure and, as target acquisition was reached, he pulled the trigger.

At that precise moment Encizo came into view, off to James's left and slightly ahead of the gunman. His finger touched the trigger of his MP-5 in the same instant James triggered his M-16.

The gunman's wild charge was abruptly terminated. He was hit by Encizo's H&K 9 mm slugs zinging from the SMG on full-auto, and also caught 3-round bursts from James's M-16. As the combined destructive power of the two weapons ripped through the man, he performed an awkward, loose-limbed death dance, turning and twisting as the hail of bullets kept him on his feet for long seconds. A fine veil of blood trailed after him as the impact of the auto blast faded and he was dumped inelegantly on the ground. Finally his last shuddering ceased, and he slipped into the stillness of death.

The crackle of gunfire drifted away and the desert land was cloaked in silence again. It remained that way for a long moment, as if even the land was drawing a reflective breath and collecting its shattered nerves in the calm following the sudden, explosive violence.

Calvin James rose to his feet, wiping a mist of sweat from his face. He walked to join Encizo where he stood over the man they had just put down. Encizo was inserting a fresh magazine into his MP-5. He slapped the mag into place with the palm of his hand, then worked the H&K's bolt, nodding to himself as it pushed the first 9 mm into the chamber.

"Feel better now?" James asked. He stood with his M-16 butted against one hip, his finger close to the trigger.

"Damn right I do!" Encizo took a deep breath, muttering something under his breath as he surveyed the killing ground. "What the hell was all this about?" he demanded.

"I'd say somebody overreacted," James remarked. "We were closer than we realized."

"Close, maybe," Encizo said, "but we still don't know where the Harrimans are being held."

"We'll check these guys over. See if they're carrying anything that might help," James suggested.

"Yes," Encizo added, "then we can give their car the same treatment."

Distasteful as it was, the searching of the bodies had to be done. Though dead men could not speak, the contents of their pockets at times provided useful information. In this instance that did not happen. The gunmen had carried nothing more than everyday items; wallets containing money, credit cards, driving licenses. Other pockets yielded cigars. A lighter. An unopened packet of condoms. But nothing indicated where the kidnap victims were being held.

"Nothing!" Encizo snapped, tossing aside a pack of chewing gum he had found. "These guys traveled heavy in hardware but light on information."

"Nobody said they had to make it easy for us, buddy," James pointed out.

"I guess not." Encizo straightened up. "Let's go check the car."

This time they hit pay dirt—in more ways than one.

9

Yakov Katzenelenbogen and Gary Manning were drinking a welcome cup of coffee in a secluded office on the United States Air Force Base in Upper Heyford, Oxfordshire. They had arrived in England a little more than thirty minutes earlier, after a six-and-a-half-hour flight from Bolling Air Force Base in a USAF Boeing C-135. They had been met off the plane by an officer from base security and driven directly to their present accommodation. Their luggage had been unloaded and had accompanied them. The security officer, Captain Dan Brenowski, had been courteous, intrigued by the clout the two VIPs obviously had, but the man remained professionally restrained. He had no doubt been given his orders concerning the Phoenix pros.

Brenowski had informed them that their liaison man from the British government was on his way and would be brought to them the moment he arrived.

"Typical." Gary Manning grinned at Katz. "We come all the way from Virginia and still get here first."

"The difference," Katz pointed out, "is that government action has to go through the machinery. We don't." He helped himself to more coffee.

"Let's hope Karl doesn't run into any red tape."

"He'll be with us when the time comes."

The door opened, and Captain Brenowski entered the room. He was followed by an athletic-looking man with dark hair and hard blue eyes.

"Gentlemen, this is Andrew Dexter," Brenowski said by way of an introduction. "You can make use of this office for as long as you wish, and leave when you are ready."

"Thank you, Captain Brenowski," Dexter said, smiling easily at the security man.

Brenowski nodded and left the room, closing the door.

"I'm sorry we couldn't have met under pleasanter circumstances," Dexter said.

"If things *were* pleasanter we wouldn't be meeting at all," Manning pointed out.

Dexter glanced at him, then murmured, "Quite."

"Has our other team member arrived?" Katz asked.

"Yes. He's been at the safehouse for a few hours."

"Good," Katz said.

"Besides setting up a safehouse, we have a vehicle at your disposal. It's outside now. For the duration of your stay I will be staying at the safehouse. I'll be on call twenty-four hours day and night. My instructions are to see you settled at the house, and also to provide you with anything you may need."

"Have there been any further developments?" Katz asked.

Dexter shook his head. "Nothing. No word from the group that took the Manta units. Nor any sightings of the units themselves."

"I don't think there will be," said Katz.

"Oh?"

"From the way this situation has developed," Katz explained, "it's looking more and more likely that these people intend to actually use the Manta missiles."

"Heavens!" Dexter whispered. From his reaction it was obvious that line of thought had not occurred to him.

"At the moment I'm relying mainly on a gut feeling," Katz explained.

"Well, it must be catching because I'm getting the same feeling," Manning said.

"Let's just hope it's nothing more than an upset from something you ate," Dexter remarked.

"I wish it was," Katz said. "Shall we go?"

Dexter nodded. He opened the door as Katz and Manning picked up their aluminum cases. Dexter had noted Katz's prosthesis, which replaced his right forearm, and had been about to offer assistance. He saw there was no need when Katz effortlessly lifted one of the cases with the steel hooks. The British liaison man led the way from the building, to where a four-wheel-drive Range Rover, painted dark blue, was parked on the tarmac. Dexter opened the tailgate so Katz and Manning could stow their cases away.

Dexter climbed behind the wheel, and Gary Manning settled himself on the wide rear seat while Katz sat in the passenger seat beside Dexter. Starting the powerful, almost silent engine, Dexter glanced across at Katz.

"I was told you would be using cover names," he said.

Katz nodded. "Yes. I'm Mr. Green. My partner is Mr. Gray."

"Fine," Dexter said. "It should take us just over an hour to reach the safehouse and your Mr. Blue."

Leaving the base behind them, Dexter drove along a narrow country road until he reached the main A34. He took a right, heading in the general direction of the famous university town of Oxford with its historic buildings and churches. They passed through a mainly rural landscape, broken occasionally by clusters of houses. Their route took them to the west of Oxford, following the ring road that bypassed the city and then on to a four-lane stretch of about twenty-five miles that brought them to the six-lane M4 motorway heading east toward London. Once on the M4 Dexter put his foot down, and the Range Rover surged forward, easily exceeding the seventy-mile-per-hour speed limit.

"We have a secure telephone link with your man in Washington," Dexter informed Katz.

Katz simply nodded. He was using the journey to relax, building his reserves of stamina for what lay ahead. Phoenix Force missions, however well-intentioned at the outset, had a tendency to go hard very early in the game. The pace of the mission was fast and generally continued to be to the bitter end. Once the action started life became intense and highly charged, leaving little time for R and R. It paid to rest wherever and whenever the opportunity presented itself, because it might be some time before another chance occurred. Knowing that, the battle-hardened Phoenix warriors conserved their energies before putting themselves on the line. Any combat soldier does the same thing. Given a lull in a battle, the combat veteran first sees to his weapons, then to himself. He eats if there is food available and rests if he isn't on duty. It is pure and simple survival technique. The stress of combat eats away a man's physical and mental reserves, so building those reserves becomes as necessary as replenishing ammunition stocks before plunging into battle.

Dexter sensed the Phoenix pair wanted this moment of calm. He was no stranger to combat situations himself, though it had been some years since his involvement. There is though, an affinity between men who have experienced combat. They recognize their own kind, and that recognition imparts the knowledge of what is important. So appreciating that Katz and Manning were taking rest time, Dexter left them alone and concentrated on the drive to London.

The motorway was quiet, traffic moderate, and Dexter found he was making good time. As they neared London, they passed by Windsor, and a little while later, to the south, the giant passenger jets were visible as they plied their way skyward from Heathrow International Airport. Toward the end of the motorway the greenery gave way to high office blocks and hotels. The trappings of a busy and densely populated major city began to close in around them. Eventually the M4 rose on concrete stilts to become an elevated highway and finally sloped down to its end in the Chiswick area of the city.

Dexter cut onto the Great West Road, then they rolled alongside the historic River Thames as they cruised through Hammersmith. Traffic began to build up on the Kensington Road, and Dexter had to slow to a crawl in places. They passed Kensington Gardens and Hyde Park, famous for its Serpentine Lake. The park itself had originally belonged to Westminster Abbey until King Henry VIII, in the years 1536 to 1539, decreed the dissolution of the monasteries, driving away the monks and claiming the lands of the Roman Catholic Church. Taking a left around the edge of Hyde Park, Dexter drove up Park Lane then along the Bayswater Road. Ten minutes later he pulled the Range Rover onto a quiet residential street. Detached private houses, each in its own walled-off grounds with heavily foliaged gardens in the back and front, lined each side of the street. Turning the Range Rover in at one of the houses, Dexter came to a stop before the pillar-flanked front doors.

The house was set back from the street. It stood three stories high, with a brick double garage extending from one side. The garage doors were partway open, and a gray Ford Granada 2.5 liter could be seen inside.

"End of the line," Dexter said.

"I hope there's somebody at home," Gary Manning commented as he waited for Katz to climb out. Tilting the front seat, the Canadian eased himself out, stretching his stiff body.

Katz had gone to the rear of the Range Rover, where he raised the tailgate door. Manning joined him and they unloaded their gear.

The Phoenix warriors followed Dexter inside. The Briton led them across a tiled entrance hall and up the carpeted stairs. At the top he led the way along a passage, pausing at a door. He tapped on it, then pushed it open.

The room was large and spacious. It was tastefully decorated and furnished. There was a large television set in one corner, complete with VCR. One wall was lined with shelves containing books and video and music cassettes. Placed around a large coffee table were comfortable leather armchairs, and seated in one of the chairs was a man whom Katz and Manning recognized immediately.

Karl Hahn.

Formerly a GSG-9 operative, Hahn had been recruited by the BND, West Germany's federal intelligence service, and trained for covert assignments in East Germany and Czechoslovakia. When he first met and worked with Phoenix Force, Hahn had been stationed in Turkey.

The BND had gained Hahn after the German's dismissal from GSG-9, due to a personal vendetta in which he had hunted down and executed eight Red Army Faction terrorists. Hahn's terrorist hunt had been triggered by the capture and torture of a close GSG-9 friend, Klaus Hausberg. Hahn's past record of exceptional service had not saved him; he had operated against Baader-Meinhof, the Second June Movement and active Palestinian terrorist groups. In 1977 Karl Hahn had been among GSG-9 operatives who carried out the now famous rescue mission against hijackers holding eighty-six hostages in a Lufthansa Boeing 747 in Mogadishu, Somalia.

Working with the BND gave Hahn invaluable experience. He already spoke three languages fluently and had a working knowledge of Czech and Russian. As an exchange student during his college years, he had studied computer electronics at UCLA.

Phoenix Force had first asked Hahn to assist them during a mission against the KGB in Turkey, and after that he had stepped in to replace Rafael Encizo when the Cuban warrior had been wounded by ODESSA Nazis during a firefight on a mission in France. Since then Hahn had joined Phoenix Force on a number of assignments.

Gary Manning put down the case and canvas duffel bag he was carrying and held out a big hand to Hahn. "Great to see you again, Blue," he greeted the BND man.

Hahn grasped the offered hand. "Glad to help."

Katz turned to Dexter. "We'd appreciate some coffee."

Dexter smiled. The request for coffee was a polite way of asking him to leave Phoenix Force alone for a while. "I'll go and arrange it," he said, and left the room.

"Hello, Karl," Katz said, glad to drop the cover names for a while.

"Yakov."

"How much do you know about the mission?" Katz asked, as they sat down in the leather armchairs.

"Only that it concerns a top-secret project named Manta and the kidnapping of someone involved with it," Hahn said.

"All right, Karl, I'll expand that for you." Katz detailed the framework of the assignment they were now handling. He included David McCarter's involvement.

Hahn listened intently, and when Katz had finished, he leaned back in his armchair, deep in thought. "I think I'd have to agree with your assessment, Yakov," he said. "These people wouldn't have gone to all the trouble of kidnapping Harriman and his family if all they were after was money for the Mantas' return. Taking the only man capable of breaking the computer access codes suggests they want to use Manta."

"Even if they do access the controls, they're still left with an unarmed missile," Manning reminded them.

"Nuclear warheads *can* be obtained," Karl said. "If they can't be stolen, they can be manufactured."

"If you're correct, we could be in for a hard time," Manning said.

"I think a hard time is what these terrorists want us to have," Katz replied. "David's late friend, Tasker, reported that his RBP contact said something about waiting for the Manta to fall. The wording may be a little flowery, but I think it implies that these people do intend using the Mantas. What we don't know is the target or the date."

"And that is what we have to find out?" asked Hahn.

"That and where the missiles are."

"So where do we start?" asked Manning.

"First we collect David from his hotel. Get him back here." Katz sat upright. "Gary, I'd like you and Karl to handle that. Take the Range Rover and pick David up now."

Manning nodded. He rose to his feet, simultaneously opening his jacket to take out his Desert Eagle .357 Magnum and check that it was loaded.

"Here's the location of David's hotel, and the room number." Katz passed a slip of paper to Manning.

"Okay," Manning said, glancing at the address. "I'll ask Dexter for a telephone number we can use to call you if we need to."

Hahn, reholstering his Walther P-5, said, "I already have it. Dexter gave it to me shortly after I arrived."

"All right, Karl," Manning said, "let's go and pick up the boy wonder."

10

The room where David McCarter was held had not
been designed or built as a prison cell, but it certainly
qualified as one. It was about twelve feet square, with
a high ceiling, which had a two-foot-square skylight.
The skylight had tough, wired glass in the frame and
provided the only illumination. The walls and floor
were bare and constructed of concrete. Access to the
room was by a pair of heavy doors, now securely
closed, which could only be opened from the outside.

Having inspected the room inch by inch, and finally having decided there was no way out except
through the door, McCarter sat down on the floor
with his back to the wall, and waited.

Sooner or later they were going to come for him.
They would ask questions they wanted answers to, and
there might be an opportunity for McCarter to break
free then. A lot would depend on how many of the
opposition were around at the time.

Given the chance, McCarter knew he would take it.
The gamble was with his own life, he knew, and he
accepted that. He was aware that his future was in the
balance. Once he had undergone questioning and his
usefulness had been exhausted, McCarter would become a liability to his captors. They would take the
easy option and kill him. If he died, so would any in-

formation he might have picked up from Jake Tasker. Tracks had to be covered, loose ends secured.

McCarter felt sure there was something heavy about to go down. His earlier contact with this RBP bunch had convinced him of that. Their efforts to silence Jake Tasker and himself certainly seemed frantic, with an air of urgency about them. No one went to such lengths unless they had something big to hide.

It was all tied in with Manta, whatever that was. Even Hal Brognola had reacted when McCarter had dropped the name. He wondered briefly just what Manta was. Being who he was, McCarter didn't dwell on the matter for long. He would learn soon enough, so there was no profit in wasting time worrying about it now.

His main concern was getting himself free and contacting Phoenix Force. He was sure they would be in England already. Maybe they had gone to his hotel to pick him up, only to find him gone. That would alert them directly to the likelihood of intervention by a third party. Despite his reckless and often flippant nature, McCarter knew when to stop the horseplay and follow orders. Brognola had told him to stay put in his room until Phoenix Force made contact. The only reason McCarter would have left under his own steam would have been if the hotel had caught fire.

Knowing that McCarter had probably been taken by force would not help his partners. McCarter was the only Phoenix Force member to have had any contact with the RBP freaks. His buddies hadn't. It didn't create an impossible situation—just a difficult one. There were always solutions to problems. It was just that some solutions took longer to arrive at than others.

McCarter was not sure how much time any of them had.

He felt his jacket, knowing before he did that he wasn't going to find anything. His abductors had emptied his pockets, taking every item they found. And that had included McCarter's cigarettes. He longed for a Player's. Come to think of it, he could have knocked back an iced Coke.

There was a rattle beyond the doors. One of them swung open, and a group of men filed into the room.

First was the American who had been in McCarter's room at the hotel. A short, stocky man dressed in a dark suit followed next. His bald head, hard, piggy eyes, made McCarter put him down straightaway as a nasty piece of work. A little way behind was a lean figure dressed in a smart suit and white shirt. The leering expression on his pale face and a wildness in his dead eyes that almost screamed the word *fanatic*. Close to the door stood a watchful hardguy carrying an SMG.

McCarter let them draw near, making no attempt to stand up. His attitude seemed to annoy the man in the suit and white shirt. He scowled at McCarter, like a little boy suddenly falling out with his ordered world.

"Get up," he yelled. "On your feet, you degenerate."

McCarter ignored him, which only increased the fanatic's fury. He thrust a long finger in McCarter's direction.

"He needs teaching a lesson, Manson. Show him who's in charge."

It was the American who was called Manson. He glanced at the fanatic and said, "Back off, Harrap. We all know who the headman is." As he spoke he offered a sly, sideways glance at the bald man, who gave a thin smile.

McCarter watched it all closely, his mind storing the details. The guy in the trendy suit obviously figured he was the top man. And while Manson and the bald man appeared to acknowledge that fact, they obviously had other ideas.

Manson turned his attention to McCarter. "Question time," he said. "You feeling cooperative?"

"Depends on the questions," McCarter answered.

"Your interference has cost us men and time," Manson said.

McCarter shrugged. "That's tough on you."

"Think so?"

"Look," McCarter said. "You kicked the whole thing off trying to take Jake Tasker outside the pub. What was I expected to do? Let it happen? He was a pal."

"And you just happened to be there?"

"If it's really any of your business—yes, I did just happen along. I dropped by the pub for a drink and Jake walked in."

Harrap gave a shrill laugh. "He's lying, Manson. He's a damn spy. Sent by the police." He stared at McCarter. "An establishment lackey. A capitalist thug."

McCarter could barely hold back a chuckle. "*Capitalist thug?* Where the hell do you get dialogue like that?"

Manson turned to Harrap. "Back off, Vern," he said calmly. "Let me do the job I'm best at."

Harrap opened his mouth to argue but decided against it. There was something about the way Manson was looking at him that cautioned him to abandon any thoughts of standing up to the man. "Oh, you go ahead, Manson," he said lightly. "I have other things to attend to." Harrap turned away and hurried out of the room.

"Asshole!" Manson murmured softly, but not so low that McCarter couldn't hear.

"I think I'd agree with you there," the Phoenix warrior said in a conversational tone.

Manson swung around on him, his eyes hard and cold. "Don't screw me around, mister," he snapped. His tone was hard, though the words were delivered precisely. McCarter was convinced the man was not fooling. "By rights you should be dead. That can still be arranged if I don't get the information I need."

"Manson, there isn't a damn thing I have to tell you," McCarter said.

"I think there is. You spent time with Tasker before he died. Enough time for him to have passed on to you what he'd picked up about us."

"What would that be?" McCarter asked innocently. "You don't mean to tell me you've been up to something illegal?" McCarter shook his head in mock disgust.

Manson suddenly drove the toe of his shoe hard into McCarter's side. Pain flared over McCarter's ribs, and the impact made him slide along the wall. Manson lunged forward, grabbing McCarter's coat and hauling the Phoenix pro to his feet. He slammed his fist into McCarter's body, then backhanded him across the side of the head. McCarter's skull bounced against the wall. There was a solid whack as Manson slugged McCarter across the jaw, tearing the flesh. Blood welled up instantly from the wound.

"You son of a bitch, you'll tell me or—"

The stocky bald man reached out to touch Manson's arm.

"You are allowing yourself to be led, Alex," he said calmly. "Don't lose control. The interrogator should always be in command of the situation."

Manson drew back, breathing deeply. His eyes never left McCarter's face.

McCarter drew a pained breath. He wiped away the blood smearing his jaw, and forced a grin onto his face.

Manson's nostrils flared. Then he mentally backed off, refusing to be intimidated by McCarter's stubborn resistance. His anger subsided.

"It is obvious that our friend here is no stranger to this kind of situation," the bald man said. "We are dealing with a professional, Alex."

"Not me, guv," McCarter pleaded in his best East End accent. "I'm just an ordinary bloke."

The bald man smiled. He seemed genuinely amused. "My name is Lubichek," he announced. "I am a professional myself, and I can recognize another pro anytime."

"That supposed to make me feel better?" McCarter asked.

Lubichek's smile broadened. "It is supposed to make you aware of your position."

"Oh, it has," McCarter said. "And right this minute my position is bloody uncomfortable. Can't you give a guy a chair to sit on?"

"I think we are all impressed by your heroics," Lubichek said. "However, being a funnyman will not stop the pain once we become serious."

"You clowns kill me," McCarter sneered. "Playing your bloody childish games. If you figure I've got information you want, you'll have to beat it out of me. And then it might not be the truth.''

"A very effective little speech," Lubichek said. "It changes nothing. One way or another we have to find out if Tasker passed any damaging information to you."

"How did you find out where I was staying?" McCarter asked, surprising Manson into answering.

The American smiled. "Surely you can guess."

"Indulge me," McCarter urged.

"When our people got to Tasker's hotel after you pulled him out of the pub attack, one of them recognized your car. It only took a few seconds to stick a homing bug under your rear bumper. We had a backup car in the area, and he just followed your signal. They saw what you did to our first team on the motorway and decided to hang back rather than risk another confrontation there and then. Your signal led them to your hotel. When you pulled into the car park, one of the men went inside the hotel by the street entrance. He was waiting when you came up from the car park. All he had to do was listen and watch. When he left the hotel he had your room number and your name—David McCarter."

"Very good," McCarter said. "So now we've all been introduced, can we finish up? I think I want to be alone again."

"You persist in maintaining this flippant attitude," Lubichek interrupted. "I do not understand."

"It's a British tradition, Comrade," McCarter explained. "Always remain cool, calm and funny in a desperate situation. Helps to break the ice and keep things on a friendly basis. Probably something you can't grasp. Always been a fault of your crowd, Ivan.

The KGB never has had much of a sense of humor.'' McCarter caught the thin ripple of anger that crossed Lubichek's face. "Of course you don't have all that much to smile about, do you?"

"What makes you imagine I am involved with the KGB?" Lubichek asked.

"That accent of yours has to be Russian. And only the KGB could be involved in a caper like this."

Lubichek stayed silent, his only reaction the slightest shrug of his shoulders.

"Come off it," McCarter protested. He watched both Manson and Lubichek as he dropped his ace card. "You lot are up to your necks in this Manta deal."

Manson, unaware that the Phoenix veteran was playing a bluff, couldn't quite hide that he was taken aback by McCarter's knowledge.

Lubichek gave little away. He studied McCarter closely, and it was obvious that he was debating whether his captive's statement was for real, or simply a stab in the dark. "Now you are playing a dangerous game," the Russian said at length.

McCarter held his icy stare. "So are you, chum. One that could blow up in your face."

The expression was a pure throwaway. But when Manson caught the words "blow up" he grabbed Lubichek's arm and drew him to the far side of the room, where the pair of them spoke together in muted tones.

McCarter realized he had inadvertently touched on a sensitive area and that he might have placed himself closer to the firing line. He began to accept the possibility that his captors might decide they would be better off if he were dead very soon. That thought alone prompted McCarter toward hard thinking on ways of getting out of the place—and the sooner the better.

Manson and Lubichek ended their discussion. The American left the room without a backward glance, and Lubichek walked across the room to confront McCarter.

"I believe you are a clever man, McCarter," he said. "What I am not certain of is just how clever. Do you really have information about our business—or are you merely bluffing? How should I react? Eliminate you here and now without full knowledge of how deeply involved you might be? Or do I keep you alive so I can determine how much you may have passed on to others?"

"Decisions," McCarter said. "It's hell at the top, Comrade."

Lubichek glanced over his shoulder and signaled the armed man at the door. "You'll come with me, McCarter," he said. "There is something I have to show you. By the way, no foolish moves. Henderson, here, will shoot without hesitation if you try anything. He won't kill you, but he will cripple you."

Lubichek led the way out of the room and along a bare, dirty passage. The floor was littered with rubbish. The building, wherever it was located, was obviously unused. It had the bleak walls and cement floors of an industrial complex, which meant they could be anywhere in or around the London area.

A flight of stairs took them to an upper floor and along yet another passage, with doors leading off on either side. Lubichek stopped at a door, he pondered a key and unlocked it. Pushing it open, he motioned for McCarter to step inside.

A naked low-wattage bulb hanging from the ceiling lit the interior. There was a hard-backed chair and a low bed, and McCarter saw that someone was lying on the bed facedown. A single window seemed to have served the room, but it was securely boarded up.

"A fellow captive," Lubichek said. "He also has information we need. Like you he is stubborn. Unlike you, he has been with us for some time and has been receiving persuasive treatment for his reluctant attitude. I will leave you alone together for a while. Give you both time to reflect on your respective positions.

"Consider one thing, McCarter. We have only a short time at our disposal. If I had more time, I would be able to employ sophisticated means for extracting information. As you yourself suspected, I am a professional. However, we are not well equipped here, and I must use primitive methods. Messy and crude—but often productive."

Lubichek pointed to the man on the bed. "You will see what I mean. Imagine it could be you and consider whether it is worth suffering for what you could tell us. Dwell on it, McCarter. Persuade each other to cooperate and let us put an end to all this nonsense."

Lubichek and the guard left the room. The door banged shut, and the key rattled in the lock.

McCarter made a swift tour of the room. The window had been sealed expertly and solidly. It would need a handyman with a set of tools to break through it, McCarter decided. The walls of the room were another matter. They were constructed of painted plasterboard panels, erected to section off individual rooms. Probably offices. McCarter leaned his weight against the closest wall and pushed. The partition gave a little. McCarter smiled. This could be his way out.

First things first. He crossed to the bed and leaned over the still form. The man stirred as McCarter touched him.

"Come on, chum, we haven't got all day."

The figure rolled over, eyes staring up at McCarter from a mask of bloodied, battered flesh. Evidently somebody had been using the man's face for a punching bag. His features were badly swollen, and gashes showed over both cheekbones and along the left jawline. His lips had been split in a number of places. Blood had spilled from his crushed nose, drenching the crumpled shirt to the waist.

"Been a rough day for you by the looks of it," McCarter said in sympathy.

The man sat up. He did it with great difficulty, holding his sides as he moved. "Bastards!" he mumbled.

"Describes them pretty well," McCarter agreed.

"Who are you?" the man asked. "How do I know you're not one of them? This could be some damn trick to get me to cooperate."

"It could be but it isn't," McCarter said. "I'm in this up to my neck because I walked into one of their setups." He indicated his bruised, bloody face. "You think I got this shaving?"

A cautious look appeared on the man's severely bruised face. He had been through a great deal of physical hardship and was probably disoriented and unsure of who might be friend or enemy.

"I'll say this only once, because I don't have much time. Whatever you think, I'm not with them. Right now my priority is to get out of here and contact my people."

McCarter returned the man's searching gaze, then said, "You believe it, chum. Just tell me one thing. Are you anything to do with this Manta deal? I don't know what it is, just every time I mention it people jump."

Again the man studied McCarter, and then appeared to come to a decision. "I'll have to take a chance," he said. "I can't tell you anything these people don't already know, so if you are one of them it doesn't matter."

"I told you the truth," McCarter said.

"All right. My name is Phillip Harriman. Manta is the code name for a mobile missile unit and system I helped develop. It's an American-British cooperative effort. Four of the mobile units, under test here in England, were hijacked by these people. They also had me kidnapped."

"Because you worked on the project?"

Harriman nodded. "Mainly because I am the only man capable of breaking the security codes locking off the control computers and accessing the program to give launching instructions."

"They want to fire the missiles?" McCarter asked.

"I think they do."

"Are the missiles armed?"

"No."

"If they went to all the trouble of stealing them, they must have access to warheads," McCarter suggested.

"I suppose so," Harriman said. He leaned forward. "There is something else." He was beginning to speak slowly, with difficulty because of his injured mouth. "They told me they have also kidnapped my wife and daughter from our ranch in New Mexico."

"Do you think it is true?"

"They confirmed it by playing a tape of my wife and daughter talking to me over a telephone. It was them. If I don't do what they. . ."

"I can guess the rest of that little speech."

Harriman glanced at the door of the room, as if he expected it to burst open at any moment. "They say if I don't give them what they want my family will die. If I do and they use the missiles, thousands may die." Harriman shuddered. "I love my wife and daughter, but I can't allow these people to cause mass destruction. I won't."

"If I can get out of here, we can do something about these freaks," McCarter said. "Do you know where they've got the Mantas?"

"They did have them here. They showed them to me to prove they had them. I don't know if that's still true."

"Harriman, can you stall them? If I can get out and contact my people, we'll be back for you. I can't say how long it might take, but we *will* be back."

"I'll hold out," Harriman said. "The only consolation is that they can't hurt me too much, or I won't be able to handle the computer."

"But they can hurt your family," McCarter reminded him. "It's why they took them. Hurt them and they hurt you. It's the way this kind of scum operate. Terrorists will use any means to get what they want. They'll justify it with all kinds of fancy talk, but when you reach the bottom line it's just plain thuggery."

"It's abominable how they use women and children. . . ."

"It's where most decent men are vulnerable. They value the lives of the ones they love. And the terrorists know that. When innocent lives are at stake, good men *can* give up the fight.''

Harriman swore bitterly. "I'm not a man of violence," he said, "but if *I* had a gun now I'd kill every last one of them for what they're doing.''

"You leave that to the likes of me. And don't worry, these creeps will get what's coming to them," McCarter promised.

"Can you break out?" Harriman asked. He was clutching his hurt body now, obviously still in pain.

McCarter grinned confidently. "If I can't, I'll hand in my badge."

"Then go ahead," Harriman urged, "before they come back."

McCarter returned to the dividing wall. He put his shoulder to it and applied pressure. The plasterboard wall flexed. Stepping back McCarter inspected the partition, running his hands over the surface until he found a section where individual panels butted together. He put his shoulder to this section and pushed hard. The resistance was less here. As he felt the wall give, McCarter increased the pressure. The plasterboard began to creak. A thick crack appeared above McCarter's head. He planted his feet against the floor and threw his shoulder against the wall again. The crack extended to floor level. Sweat beaded McCarter's face as he kept up the pressure. His ribs ached where Manson had kicked him, but he closed his mind to the pain. The wall's cracking increased, and the edge of one panel gave way. McCarter concentrated his efforts on that section. Gradually the panel started to part from its neighbor, and a narrow gap started to show. McCarter had to ease off then.

Taking a moment to rest he once more inspected the damaged wall. The broken panel had been pushed back about six inches along one edge. He placed a foot against it, felt it give a little more. Estimating that the panel would break free if he hit it hard enough, he backed up, bracing himself, then launched his body forward. His left shoulder struck the edge of the panel with his full weight behind it. The impact jarred him, then the panel seemed to collapse inward and fell away.

His momentum took him through the gap, into the adjoining room. The Phoenix warrior skidded across the floor in a shower of plaster debris. He tucked his shoulder in as he hit the floor in a forward roll that brought him to his feet again.

McCarter turned and saw with relief that the wood-framed window in this room had not been boarded up. He crossed to it, peering through the dirty glass. There was a flat roof about eight feet below. He reached for the catch.

From behind him came the crash of a door being kicked open. Light spilled into the room, and McCarter hastily twisted away from the window.

The guard who had been outside Harriman's door burst in, his SMG's muzzle tracking around the room to pick up David McCarter.

11

The hardguy stormed into the room head-on!

He didn't take time to assess the situation. His eyes were still searching the room when McCarter hit him full tilt. The Phoenix commando had hurled himself across the width of the room, and his solid weight was behind the body slam that spun the hardguy off balance, smashing him into the wall. The impact ripped a surprised grunt from the guy's throat. McCarter didn't give him the opportunity to even think about fighting back. He smashed a clenched fist into the unprotected stomach, driving the breath from the man's body, leaving him choking for air. Then a roundhouse punch drove him to his knees, blood streaming from his mouth. As the hardguy's head sank to his chest McCarter slammed the toe of his shoe into the exposed skull. It connected with a crunch, whipping the guard's head against the wall. The hardguy suddenly became very soft and crumpled in a heap.

McCarter reached down and snatched the SMG from limp fingers. It was a 9 mm Uzi. He quickly frisked the guard and located two extra 32-round magazines. He dropped these in his coat pocket.

In the distance McCarter heard footsteps clattering along the passage. He knew it was time he made his exit—and made it fast. He needed space to operate in. Getting pinned down in a small room was not wise practice.

His one regret was that he was unable to get Phillip Harriman out. McCarter knew it was both impossible and impractical. Harriman excelled in mental agility, not the physical kind. He was a man who worked with his brain. He was not trained in the rough-and-tumble of McCarter's world. Even if he had been in good shape, his reflexes would have been way behind those of McCarter. In the split-second timing of close-quarter combat situations Harriman was probably a child among men. But he was in less than good shape. The beating he had been subjected to had slowed his reaction time. Harriman wouldn't be able to keep up with McCarter, with the end result that both would be recaptured.

As much as he disliked the thought, McCarter was aware that the best he could do was to get out himself and return with Phoenix Force.

The pounding sound of footsteps was getting louder, accompanied by voices raised in anger. McCarter took a run at the window, thrusting the SMG ahead of him.

He launched himself through the window. Wood and glass splintered, exploding outward along with McCarter's taut form. He saw the surface of the flat roof rushing up to meet him, and relaxed his body, allowing it to curl up loosely as he struck the roof. He rolled, absorbing the impact, then slithered to a stop, getting his balance before bounding up and sprinting the length of the roof.

The harsh crackle of automatic fire opened up. Hot slugs peppered the roof around him, blasting chunks of black tar into the air. McCarter kept moving, taking a zigzag route in order to present a difficult target. More weapons opened up, making the air around him hum with potential death. Somebody was expanding a lot of ammunition to try and stop him.

The end of the roof came in sight. Reaching it, McCarter dropped flat and peered over the edge. It was twelve or thirteen feet to the concrete below. Rolling over on his side, he brought his borrowed Uzi around and leveled it at the approaching gunners. He loosed off a long burst.

The 9 mm parabellums made the RBP men scatter. McCarter's aim was deadly accurate, and one guy went down clutching his middle as red-hot tumblers opened his flesh. A second man caught a hail of lead in the throat and died in a wash of hot blood.

McCarter knew he had only seconds before the scattered gunners regrouped and came on. He swung his legs over the edge of the roof, letting his body follow. Holding the Uzi in his left hand, he gripped the rough edge of the asphalt roof and lowered himself to arm's length. Without hesitation he let himself drop, pushing away from the wall. He landed hard with bent knees to reduce the shock.

He took swift stock of his position and surroundings. The first thing he noticed was the failing light. Dusk was fast approaching—which meant it had to be around 9:00 p.m. The coming darkness would help to conceal his escape.

From his position McCarter saw a spread of empty, derelict buildings. Piles of rubble and tangled webs of steelwork made it evident he was in some disused industrial complex. An abandoned, desolate place where he was not likely to find many friends.

His priority was to evade capture and get to a telephone. If he could get through to Brognola, the Fed could patch him through to Phoenix Force.

Only seconds had passed since he had dropped from the roof and it was time for McCarter to break away from the side of the building. He took no more than a dozen steps before a chattergun opened up. The concrete around him cracked and splintered as high-velocity slugs whacked against it. McCarter felt ragged chips of concrete tug at his pants and bounce off his shoes.

He spun round, his Uzi tracking in on the RBP gunman blasting away at him. For the second time McCarter showed them how it should be done. A hail of bullets from his Uzi made his opponent plunge off the roof to hit the concrete headfirst with a sickening crack.

On the move again, McCarter caught movement off to his right. A group of men had come boiling out of a ground-level door and started in hot pursuit of their escaping prisoner. Although they were armed with automatic weapons, they were not trained in combat techniques, being mainly hard-core street thugs whose main experience was with handguns. There was more to firing the Uzi than simply aiming and pulling the trigger. The 9 mm SMG was capable of spitting out death at a cyclic rate of six hundred rounds per minute. In the hands of an inexperienced gunner the Uzi could exhaust its magazine in seconds. Spraying an area with bullets looked and sounded impressive, and might have worked for Rambo on screen. In reality it didn't add up to much when the object was to hit the target.

Uncoordinated firing loosed off a wild swarm of bullets that clanged off steelwork or bit chunks out of the concrete. McCarter dodged behind a pile of rubble as the bunch of gunners swept up on him. He heard the whack and whine of slugs bouncing off the broken bricks and lumps of shattered concrete. A few stray brick splinters stung his face.

From his coat McCarter plucked one of the spare 9 mm mags. He ejected the partly used mag and snapped in the fresh one. Then he crouch-walked to the far end of the pile of rubble, working his way around the outer edge. He was able to view the advancing gunners from the side and track them with the Uzi.

One of the RBP men turned his head and spotted McCarter. At the warning yell the whole group began to turn in McCarter's direction.

But McCarter didn't allow them time to complete the move. He triggered the Uzi, hosing them with well-directed 9 mms.

As the RBP goons retreated, McCarter ripped off another burst aimed at their midst, then turned on his heel and raced away. He was heading for another empty building, hoping to fend off his pursuers until full darkness afforded him total cover. After that he hoped to slip away and follow through with his plans.

Time was critical. The hijackers were going to move from this location to another base. And when they did go, they would take Phillip Harriman with them. The more McCarter thought about it, the more certain he became that the RBP would have a safe site at another location. The problem would be finding it. There was no need to base the missiles close to any target. The Manta missiles only had to be programmed and launched, and they would seek out their target.

The Phoenix commando ducked low as he ran inside the cavernous structure that looked as if it had served as a vast storage warehouse. Now it was a gloomy, dusty shell with empty rows of high shelving. Pools of water spread across the floor where rain had leaked in through gaps in the roof.

McCarter dashed along row after row of shelving, making for the far side of the warehouse, seeking an exit, even while he heard his pursuers crash noisily into the building. McCarter shook his head at their clumsiness. One thing for sure—they were never going to sneak up on him unawares.

He took cover behind a thick, upright support girder, his eyes probing the lengthening shadows. He saw the scurrying shapes of the advancing gunners. McCarter flicked the Uzi's selector to single shot. He raised the weapon, sighting swiftly as one of the RBP goons broke free from a patch of shadow. He waited until the guy was in the open, tracking his movement, then squeezed the trigger. The Uzi cracked out its shot. The lone 9 mm parabellum flashed through the gloom. It punched its way through the target's left eye and drilled through the skull.

A second, then a third man showed, blasting away with their SMGs. McCarter dropped to a crouch as bullets whizzed by him or clanged against the steel girder, howling off into the gathering gloom.

"Okay, boys, come and get it!" McCarter murmured. His Uzi cracked twice more, and the RBP pair were swept off their feet to end up lying on the ground like broken bloodied dolls.

McCarter broke cover, continuing his run through the empty warehouse. He knew that more RBP gunmen would soon take up the chase. At the far side of the warehouse the Phoenix hardguy spotted a door that was partway open. He eyed it with suspicion. It looked too easy. Tempting. He resisted and glanced along the wall where he saw a window some eighteen feet to his left. When he reached it, he carefully freed the catch. The window's frame swung inward. McCarter stepped over the sill and found himself outside the warehouse, facing in the direction of the door he had just declined to use.

Three armed figures were waiting to one side of the door, waiting to ambush him as he came through. McCarter smiled grimly to himself. He returned the fire selector on his Uzi to full-auto, swept the barrel around and pulled the trigger.

A red-hot burst of 9 mm manglers flew through the gap between McCarter and the trio of fanatics. Flesh disintegrated under the impact with spurtings of blood. The ambushers briefly jerked and twitched in protest against the pain and the rapid approach of death.

McCarter ran to where they lay in pools of their own blood. He scanned their weapons. All had been carrying Uzi 9 mms. He grabbed two of the weapons, then raced off into the enveloping darkness, away from the complex of buildings and toward a straggling line of trees that seemed to mark the boundary of the vast industrial site. As he ran, McCarter ejected the mags from the two Uzis he had picked up. He tossed the weapons aside and dropped the mags into his coat pocket.

Just before he reached the tree line he heard the rising growl of car engines. Over his shoulder he saw two dark sedans careering across the uneven ground, the beams of their headlights rising and falling. The chase, he realized, was far from over.

McCarter threw himself down in the thick grass that grew around the trees. Moments later the beams of the headlights bounced off the trunks of the trees, only a foot or so above his head. The cars then came to a rocking halt, the doors swinging open as the occupants leaped out.

The moment he had hit the ground McCarter twisted his body so as to face the oncoming cars. The glare of the headlights created a wall of illumination, and McCarter knew he had to do something about those lights that virtually pinned him down.

Even as the thought raced through his mind, he acted on it. He swung the Uzi up and sent a burst of 9 mm parabellums in the direction of the cars. Raking the muzzle back and forth, he extinguished the lights in a shower of broken glass. Angry shouts followed the crackle of gunfire.

As the night was plunged back into darkness, McCarter sprang to his feet. Bullets thudded into the trunks as he weaved his way through the trees.

Without warning McCarter emerged into open ground. Some fifty feet away was a sagging chain-link fence, and beyond lay a road.

The ground underfoot was soft and waterlogged, slowing his progress. He pushed on, ignoring the pulse of pain in his side and focusing his attention on the fence. If he could reach it and survive being exposed as he climbed over it, then his chances were much improved.

Autofire split the night wide open. Bullets plowed into the ground all around him, followed by a sudden, shocking burst of pain across his left shoulder. The solid impact knocked him off balance, and he sprawled in the clinging mud.

McCarter ignored the keen pain engulfing his shoulder. Twisting over onto his back, he shoved himself to a sitting position. He was not ready to lie down and die. What he was, instead, was bloody angry.

A wild, exhilarating fury swept over him. He tracked the Uzi round, picking up the shadowy figures rushing across the open ground toward him.

McCarter opened fire, letting the Uzi spit out its stream of death dealers in a continuous burst. The burning 9 mms found their targets and ripped the life from them. Blood and flesh filled the night air. Men screamed as the white-hot life stealers drilled into them, rupturing vital organs and shattering bones.

Ejecting the spent magazine, McCarter snatched a fresh one from his coat and jammed it into place. He racked back the bolt, chambering the first round. He climbed to his feet.

Off to his right another RBP goon was desperately reloading but had no time left as McCarter blew him off his feet.

Gritting his teeth against the pain but feeling there were no pursuers left, McCarter trudged to the fence. He kicked aside a broken section of fencing and slithered down the bank of earth. In the shadows he reloaded the Uzi again, then concealed it under his coat as he moved off along the road. His shoulder was aching fiercely, and there was a warm and steady flow of blood down his back and chest.

The road curved up ahead. Approaching it, McCarter stayed in the shadows at the side. Around him were more industrial sites, mostly deserted, the buildings dark and derelict. A few had security lights shining in their compounds.

Rounding the bend, McCarter saw a junction, where a main road intersected the service road he was on. Vehicles sped along the main road, and McCarter headed for it.

All he needed now was to find a telephone.

12

Alex Manson viewed the escape of the man as a minor annoyance. Arrangements were already in hand for the evacuation of the first base. Relocation at the operation center had been planned from the start, and the move, well under way when McCarter had appeared on the scene, continued.

McCarter's escape had caused some panic among the RBP rank and file, but Manson had gathered the group and had given them a rallying speech.

First he had kicked ass at their clumsy performance. Letting *one* man escape and at the same time losing so many of their group. They had, he'd yelled, let the RBP down. Even given their superior numbers and excellent weapons, they had failed. Running around in the shadows like witless chickens, blasting away without thought. He reminded them of the time he and Kovic and Landis had spent showing them the right way to handle themselves and their weapons.

Then he had questioned their loyalty to the RBP. Were they really committed? Or were they just barroom loyalists—full of bravado when they were full of drink? Hadn't he, Manson, and his men put themselves fully behind the party, deserting the United States military machine for something they felt was better? It was a chance to hit back at the capitalist warmongers who had enslaved a gullible world. The ideals of the RBP were worth fighting for. It was a chance to eliminate the ruling class who were holding down the proletariat and refusing to allow them to advance themselves. The time for attack was now. When the battle had been won and the RBP emerged victorious, peace loving nations the world over would see the freedom fighters of the party as heroes. Heroes of the revolution.

They had loved every word he spoke.

Manson had felt ten feet tall. Aware of his leadership qualities, he had momentarily forgotten the real intention of the exercise and had allowed himself to bask in the glory of his own oratory. The warmth it created had been close to sexual.

Then Manson's military discipline had taken over, and he was in control again. He let his audience off the hook by telling them that the man who had killed their friends was an example of the establishment's determination to maintain its hold on the country. He made McCarter out to be a highly trained assassin, a man totally conditioned to the peak of his abilities. He was a soulless, pitiless killing machine. He was, Manson had said, one of a squad of government-sanctioned killers who were programmed to hunt down and kill anyone not agreeing with public opinion.

Manson had reminded his audience that *they* held the whip hand. The hijacked Mantas were still theirs, and they would powerfully bolster their demands when it came time to confront and negotiate with the government.

The whole speech had been designed to ensure the continued support of the fanatic RBP members until he and Lubichek no longer needed them. No one belonging to the RBP, not even Vernon Harrap, the manic leader of the party, knew the real reason behind the Manta hijack. When the final act of the Manson–Lubichek scenario went down, it would make a lot of people stand and stare. Including the whole of the RBP.

By that time Manson and Lubichek planned to be long gone, having quietly exited by the back door. There would be no fond farewells. In truth Manson would be pleased to be rid of the RBP. They were to a man the lowest form of life to have ever been allowed to walk the streets. They were misfits and degenerates, overflowing with antisocial tendencies. They hated law and order, were unrepentantly envious of anyone with more than his share of money and possessions. They were, in fact, just the kind of fanatic to be attracted by the racist, revolutionary, anarchic rabble-rouser called Vernon Harrap. The leader of the RBP was a self-appointed father figure, who had persuaded a large number of the nation's misfits that the RBP was the savior of the working class.

Harrap was an over-the-top zealot. A man obsessed with his vision of a Marxist state replacing the old order. The man existed in a fantasy world of his own making, surrounded by his images of Marx and Lenin. He preached his brand of hard-line communism with all the fire of a wild-eyed evangelist. Harrap was the worst kind of convert. He moved in a direct line, accepting no deviation from the basic doctrine.

Even Lubichek, the KGB professional, found Harrap's eternal diatribes hard on the nerves. Lubichek had roamed the world on assignments for his KGB masters in Moscow, and he could deliver epic monologues on the credibility of Soviet policy. Yet he visually cringed when subjected to Harrap's wild rantings. The Russian was no fool. He knew that Harrap's policy for the RBP stood little chance of achieving any lasting effect. The RBP was a lunatic fringe party, too much into posturing and rallying. They advocated violence on a grand scale, radical change to excess. But they failed to live up to their manifesto.

True, they had carried out a few attacks on racist minorities and had burned a few properties. But it had only been since the tie-up with Manson and Lubichek that the RBP had been involved in a genuine act of terrorism, though even here, in hijacking the Manta missiles, they had been led and guided by Manson and his men. The bungled attempt on Jake Tasker's life had been carried out by men hired for the job by the RBP. Even during the successful second attempt the RBP had lost men when McCarter had hit back with deadly effect. And as for their performance during McCarter's escape—the less said about that the better, Manson decided.

The remainder of Harrap's followers were on their way to the main operation. Before they left, Manson had had them gather up all the discarded weapons and load them in one of the cars. The dead RBP men had been hurriedly carried off and placed without ceremony in one of the empty sheds.

Phillip Harriman, under close guard, was in one of the cars.

All that remained was for Manson to make a quick telephone call to his ex-sergeant and fellow deserter, Ron Kovic, who was in residence at the RBP headquarters in London.

Manson stared thoughtfully into space until the telephone's summons was answered. "Ron? We're moving out now. Stick around where you are for a while. The guy we took out of the hotel broke out a while back. That's why we're getting out earlier than planned. When he finds us gone he could try your place. If he does, try and keep him occupied for as long as you can before you get out. It'll give us a clear chance to get up-country. Soon as you can, join us. See you, Sergeant."

Manson took a final look around the room that had served as their HQ during the first phase of the operation. It was time to move toward the conclusion of the plan. And what a conclusion, he thought. By God it would make them sit up in the White House and the Kremlin.

The only obstacle to overcome was Phillip Harriman's stubborn resistance. But better men than the computer genius had broken. It was very important to the plan that they had gotten hold of his family. Unquestionably, it would give them a great deal of leverage.

"Let's go," Lubichek said from the doorway.

The American renegade nodded and walked from the room to join the Russian. Together they made their way to the waiting car.

Minutes later the six cars left the desolate industrial site, driving off in pairs, a wide gap between each vehicle. Three routes had been worked out. No one was going to take much notice of two cars traveling in the same direction. The three pairs of cars would meet up again within a few miles of their destination.

Once there, the final act would commence.

13

Manning and Hahn had been gone for almost forty minutes when Dexter entered the room with a sealed envelope. He handed it to Katz.

"It came by courier from the prime minister's office," he explained. "Strictly for your attention."

Katz took the envelope and ripped it open. Inside was a closely typed sheet of paper. Katz read it slowly, absorbing every word. When he had finished, he folded the paper and returned it to the envelope. As he pocketed it, he felt Dexter's eyes on him.

The Phoenix Force commander faced the British security man. "You wouldn't want to hear what it said," he assured Dexter.

Dexter smiled ruefully. "What *do* I get to hear?"

"Right now I'd like as much information on the RBP as possible. Particularly anything on people connected with or suspected of being connected with the RBP. Everything you have."

Dexter nodded. "Give me a half hour."

Once he was alone, Katz sat down to reread the message he had received from the British prime minister. The news was not good. The contents of the message had also been relayed to the White House and Stony Man, so Brognola would be in possession of the information, as well. As Katz scanned the message he felt a chill finger work its way down his spine. It was a constant fact of life that when things were looking bad they always got worse. The Israeli commando reached for the telephone with the direct line to Brognola. As he punched out the numbers, Katz went over the message again in his mind.

Its basics were as follows: a French antiterrorist squad, after intensive investigations, had tracked down to their Paris hideout a group of terrorists belonging to the extremist Islamic Jihad Hezbollah movement. The French had stormed the house being used by the terrorists. A firefight had ensued. The six terrorists, of Tunisian origin, had all been killed. The French had lost one man, with another slightly wounded.

A searching of the house revealed weapons and ammunition in large quantities. The squad also found materials for bomb manufacturing, plus a number of completed timed devices.

In an upstairs room they found printing and copying equipment for preparing propaganda leaflets. There were also maps on which were marked locations and dates referring to where and when bombs were to be planted and exploded. Two locations were ringed in black; when the dates were checked they tallied with bombs that had already exploded. One had been in a busy supermarket and had caused the deaths of more than twenty people, the majority of them women and children. Many others had been severely wounded. The second bomb had been planted in a tourist hotel. Fortunately, an error in timing had set off the bomb when the building had been almost empty. Three had died and the hotel porter had lost a leg. The documentation found in the hideout gave the

French authorities valuable information, and from it they were able to locate and defuse three bombs already planted.

During the intensive search of the mass of documents that had been found, a file was discovered with information so shocking that it was instantly given top-secret status and rushed to the French security department. The file revealed that the terrorists had entered into a liaison with the Red Britannia Party. The Hezbollah had provided four low-yield nuclear devices that were to be smuggled into England, along with two Libyan-trained technicians. The devices were to be used in a demonstration of the RBP's power and determination to overcome the ruling class that held sway in England.

The information was in the form of a press release intended to have been sent out after the so-called demonstration. No indication of where or when the demonstration was to take place was included in the documentation.

Katz heard the electronic sound of the scramblers coming into play. After a few more soft clicks the distant telephone rang. It was picked up on the second ring and Hal Brognola spoke. "Yes?"

"Katz."

"How are things over there?"

"Gary and Karl are on their way to pick David up from his hotel."

"Good."

"Have you had the message from France?"

"Damn right," Brognola said. Katz could visualize him chewing on the end of his cigar.

"It means we really have to move fast," he said. "We don't have any idea how much time we have left."

"I wish I had more to tell you," Brognola said.

"We've worked with less, Hal," Katz reminded him.

"Yeah, I know. But I hate sending you guys out without knowing all the angles."

"Have you heard anything from Rafael and Calvin?"

"Nothing yet," Brognola said. "Katz, do you need anything?"

"Just more information on the people we're dealing with."

"You'll get anything that comes off the wire," Brognola promised.

"One more thing, Hal," Katz said. "The way the missile hijack took place. I've had time to think about it, and the way the perimeter guards had been taken out make it look like military planning more and more. Might be worthwhile checking into recent desertions, or military personnel suspected of discontent. Could be we have some renegade military types who have thrown in with the RBP."

"Will do," Brognola acknowledged. "Let me know about David when you get him back."

"All right," Katz said. He hung up, and almost immediately the instrument began to ring. He snatched it up.

"Blue here," came Karl Hahn's voice.

"Green," Katz replied. "Go ahead."

"He isn't here," Hahn said. "His luggage is but the room is empty."

"Damn!" Katz muttered. "Did you find anything?"

"Couple of bloodstains on the carpet near the bed. They were not very old. And the lock on the door looks like it may have been forced."

"No one saw anything?"

"Nothing. It is a large hotel. As far as the desk is concerned, they were following instructions not to disturb Mr. White," Hahn said, using McCarter's cover name.

"For sure he was taken by force, given his previous experience," Katz said.

"I don't think he left voluntarily, either," Hahn added. "We checked the car park and his hire vehicle is still there. Looks like somebody has been trying to compact it."

"Collect his luggage," Katz said. "Settle with the desk and get back here as fast as you can."

"Will do," said the German ace and cut the connection.

Katz shook his head. It was logical to assume David had been taken by the RBP. They would be anxious to learn if he had been given any information by the late Jake Tasker. With the way things were developing, the RBP had a lot to hide. They would be desperate to learn if there had been any leaks. But the RBP would be fighting a losing battle if they tried to extract it from the British Phoenix warrior. Katz knew McCarter well. Despite his touchy nature the Briton was a genuine hardguy. It wasn't in his makeup to give anything away, especially under duress.

Still, Katz was concerned because McCarter was more than just a member of Phoenix Force. He was a friend, a man who had sided with Katz on many occasions. Too much had passed between them. There was no way Katz could *not* be worried. Katz paced the room, his mind racing. Where to start to find McCarter. There was a knock on the door. It was Dexter.

"Your information is being collected now," he said, then saw that Katz wasn't giving his full attention. "Has something happened?"

"Mr. Blue just called from the hotel. Our friend has disappeared."

"Your tone suggests he didn't go willingly."

"He was under orders to stay until we collected him. And he obeys orders."

"The RBP?"

"We have to assume so," Katz replied.

"We know of one place where they may have taken him," Dexter said.

"Where?"

"Their London HQ. They run the party business from a house in Islington. The neighborhood is a dump, but the RBP can pick up any number of likely recruits in the area."

"It's worth a visit," Katz said. "As soon as Mr. Blue and Mr. Green get back, we'll go for it."

"You want me along?" Dexter asked.

"If you can get us there in record time," Katz said, "you're welcome."

14

Gary Manning and Karl Hahn arrived back at the safehouse twenty minutes later. The last of the daylight had faded, and darkness cloaked the city.

Katz briefed them on the French report and on the next step slated to be carried out.

"This mission gets hotter with every turn of the card," Manning said.

"Proves your theory about the missiles being used," Hahn exclaimed.

Katz nodded. "It's one time I wish I'd been wrong."

"We ready to move?" Manning asked.

Katz nodded.

At that moment the telephone rang. Hahn, who was closest, answered the call and listened.

"What is it?" Katz asked impatiently.

Hahn held up a hand for silence. "Yes, operator, I accept the charges. Now please put the call through. Hello—*David!* Hell, guy, where are you?"

Hahn started to scribble information on a pad.

"Fine. Listen—you stay where you are and we'll pick you up shortly. What? Yes, yes, I'm sure we can." Hahn put down the receiver.

"Sure we can do what?" Manning asked.

Hahn grinned. "He wants a can of Coke put on ice."

"No doubt about it," Katz said. "That was Mc-Carter."

Dexter was called to join them.

"Change of plan," Katz said after telling him to join them. "Our kidnapped friend has broken out. He just called us and told us where to pick him up."

"He has the location of the terrorists' hideout," Hahn said.

Dexter looked impressed. "What about Harriman?"

"He was there," Hahn said.

Manning grabbed a couple of zippered carryalls and headed for the door. The others followed.

As they left the house and stepped into the warm night shadows, Dexter asked, "By the way, where are we going?"

Hahn was just settling into the rear of the Range Rover alongside Manning and said, "Rainham. There's a large industrial site, abandoned now, that was a former assembly plant for trucks. It's off the A13. The terrorists have been using it to hole up."

"I know the area," Dexter said, swinging the Range Rover out onto the street. "That whole section is waste ground and work sites."

"Our friend, Mr. White, will be waiting outside the Truckers' Rest."

Dexter smiled. "A well-known greasy spoon diner."

He gunned the vehicle along the lamplit streets. From the way he drove, making turns without hesitation, it was plain that Dexter knew his city well. He pushed the Range Rover through a maze of minor roads that eventually brought them to the Edgware Road, where they traveled for about three-quarters of a mile before taking a left that swung them by the

looming edifice of Marble Arch and on into Oxford
Street. The brightly lit windows of the famous street's
fashionable stores flashed by in a blur of neon color
as Dexter weaved his way through the traffic. They left
Oxford Street behind them, going left up Blooms-
bury Way and Theobald's Road. Dexter made a right
onto Gray's Inn Road, passing the local police station
on the corner. At the bottom he turned onto High
Holborn, speeding by the Daily Mirror building whose
many windows spilled light into the night. Over the
Holborn Viaduct, then down again, they passed by the
Central Criminal Court. As they followed the curve of
the road onto Cheapside, the towering outline of
Christopher Wren's St. Paul's Cathedral held their
attention for a few moments, then the historic building slipped behind them majestically on the right. Built
mainly out of Portland Stone, the building, to the top
of the cross on the central dome, rose 365 feet above
the city streets. The crypt of the church was the last
resting place of many historical figures, including
Nelson and Wellington, and the building was a great
tourist attraction with its famous Whispering Gallery. Not far along from St. Paul's they rolled onto
Cornhill, with the dark mass of the Bank of England
on their left, at the head of the street that had become
synonymous with the bank—Threadneedle Street,
from which the bank had gotten its affectionate title
of the Old Lady of Threadneedle Street. Up along
Aldgate High Street and they were on the A13, heading out toward Rainham. Dexter pushed hard now,
along the Commercial Road, past the East India
Docks, now dark and empty in silent remembrance of
London's seafaring era.

Dexter ignored speed restrictions and lane discipline. His foot hit the floor along with the gas pedal, and the Range Rover leaped forward. Twice he went through red lights, causing other drivers to brake fiercely and curse him long and loud. They roared along the straight road, hardly noticing the sprawling, giant Ford assembly plant at Dagenham, and zoomed by the sign that told them they had reached the Rainham district. Minutes later Dexter swung off the main road, rolling the Rover across a pitted, much-abused tarmac parking lot that held a number of semitrailers. The drivers were inside the brightly lit, low building that gaudily advertised itself as the Truckers' Rest. A jukebox pounded out loud music, the noise filtering outside to fight with the roar of passing traffic.

Dexter braked the Range Rover. They all sat in the dark cab of the vehicle, their eyes watchful. It never paid to jump into any situation until it had been fully assessed.

At the end of the building, close to where they were parked, stood a yellow British Telecom phone booth. The booth was in shadow on the side away from the road. Katz sat and watched the block of shadow for some time. He finally moved, reaching out to open his door.

"Hey!" Manning hissed.

"I'm all right," Katz assured him. "Just cover my back as a precaution."

Manning nodded, slipping his .357 Desert Eagle from its leather. Beside him Karl Hahn unlimbered his 9 mm Walther P-5.

Katz stepped from the Range Rover and moved confidently toward the dark phone booth. His hand was on the butt of his SIG-Sauer P-226. He crossed the uneven parking lot, his gaze fixed on the phone booth. When he was twenty feet from it he stopped and waited in silence.

"Remind me, Katz, I've forgotten this week's bloody password," David McCarter said from the shadows.

Katz smiled. "Clown," he said.

"It's about time you blokes got here," McCarter said with pretended sourness as he stepped away from the booth.

The revealing light spilling from the diner's windows made McCarter lower the Uzi SMG he was holding and also allowed Katz to see the Briton's condition. McCarter's clothing was torn and stained. There was a dark patch of blood marking his left shoulder, and his face was bruised and bloody.

"Are you fit to carry on, David?" Katz asked.

"Just a bit of patching up needed, Katz. But I'm hopping mad because I couldn't get Phillip Harriman out with me."

"Don't worry about that," Katz said. "Let's get moving and maybe we can still get to him."

Just before they reached the Range Rover, Katz caught McCarter's arm. "The driver is called Dexter. He's our liaison man during the mission. He's from some government department. For security reasons, though, we only tell him what *we* feel he needs to know."

"Are we using cover names?"

Katz nodded. "I'm Green. Karl is Blue and Gary is Mr. Gray."

"Me?"

"You are Mr. White this time around," Katz said.

McCarter grinned. "As pure as the bleedin' snow."

They climbed into the Range Rover and Dexter roared off into the night, taking them to their rendezvous with the unknown.

"JUST OUR BLOODY LUCK!" McCarter growled angrily. He had passed along all the information, and had led his teammates back to where he'd escaped from.

He was pacing the now empty room where he had spoken to Phillip Harriman such a short time back.

"It was to be expected they would move out," Katz said.

"Is that supposed to make me feel better?" McCarter snapped. "I was *here*. In the middle of the whole bloody bunch of them, and I couldn't do a damn thing."

"You shortened the odds quite a lot," Manning pointed out, referring to the dead RBP men they had found in one of the buildings, and Katz nodded approvingly, then turned toward Karl Hahn and Dexter who appeared in the doorway at that moment.

"I think you should come and take a look at what we found," Hahn said.

They followed Hahn through the building, out into the darkness, and across to one of the other structures. It was a long, low building. The moment they entered, the lingering smell of paint and solvents filled their nostrils. Hahn had turned on the overhead lights, flooding the interior with cold, harsh light, so they were able to see the equipment scattered about the place. A large portable compressor stood against one wall. On a cluttered bench were abandoned spray guns streaked with dried paint. Empty cans had been tossed in a corner. In another area of the building were cut pieces of aluminum sheet and alloy strips. Electric power drills and cutting tools lay on the floor. Rivets and screws were strewn across the concrete floor.

"Somebody has been busy here recently," Hahn said. "The paint runs down those cans are still soft." He smoothed out a crumpled sheet of paper he had found at the back of the bench. Someone had sketched working diagrams of long, boxlike shapes, the shape of a vehicle with an extended cab and a tube formation riding behind it. There were also measurements and calculations. "I think the Mantas were brought here after the hijack so they could be worked on. Fake container bodies were constructed to hide the missiles. Then the units were painted to conceal the olive drab. The military registration plates were replaced with civilian ones. Those missile units have been driven to another location looking just like any commercial delivery trucks you'd expect to see on the road any day. Who would notice them?"

McCarter wandered across the concrete floor, seemingly uninterested. Suddenly he lashed out with his foot at an empty paint can, sending it flying across the floor. His action expressed his frustration. There was no need for words, from McCarter or any of them . . . it was how they all felt!

15

The night was dark and seemed full of secrets, Boris Lubichek reflected as they rolled toward their up-country base. But it had been no secret that nothing would deter his progress through the ranks of the KGB. His superiors had realized very early in Lubichek's career that the stocky, only son of a farmer from an agricultural community near Minsk would give his best to the cause if he was allowed a degree of freedom lesser KGB operatives would never achieve. Lubichek was something of a loner, and that he was allowed to pursue his solitary existence was unusual in itself. The KGB, though very much a part of the ruling hierarchy in the Soviet pecking order, was fairly rigid within the confines of its insidious organization. Members of the Komitet Gosudarstvennoi Bezopasnosti were expected to toe the line without question and with unfailing loyalty. There was no room for prima donna KGB operatives.

Boris Lubichek was given an open brief, his long-term task to create and manage covert operations of terror and destruction in any given area of Soviet interest. Lubichek's natural instinct for his trade brought success after success. He gave a helping hand in many incidents over the years that ranged globally from Europe to Africa, Latin America and the United

States. He cultivated contacts within the hard-core elements of the IRA, pushing weapons and finance to the Irish terrorists so they could continue to wreak havoc on their own soil as well as the British mainland. There was the Lubichek hand in the Middle East, helping to stir the troubles in that war-torn part of the world. If a growing situation showed promise of destabilizing some regime that would benefit the Soviet cause, then Boris Lubichek could often be found manipulating those taking part, and doing it so cleverly that he would be considered an ally.

Due to his ability to change sides or character to suit any given situation, Lubichek's file at KGB headquarters overlooking Moscow's Dzerzhinsky Square, listed his code name as Chameleon. It was Lubichek's constant state of flexibility that enabled him to adapt to new situations almost at will, without in-depth consultations that could often lose an operative valuable time. Staying ahead of the game often meant the difference between winning or losing. Lubichek did not like losing, and in his business more often than not being dead was just another way of saying you had lost.

Lubichek had for some time been cultivating his connection with Vernon Harrap and the RBP, enduring Harrap's fanaticism with stoic patience. The man himself, he considered a bore. A fool as well, because he believed his brand of communism could sweep him along the political tide. Harrap was too shortsighted to see that his overzealous approach and radical thinking would appeal only to the extreme element, those who wanted to be involved in violence for its own sake. Harrap had little chance of involving anyone with serious political commitments. In fact the

British Communist party had disowned Harrap on more than one occasion. They, too, found his interpretation of Marxist ideology at odds with their own. They accused him of trying to undermine accepted party policy. Harrap in turn had denounced them, called them traitors to the cause, and accused them of having set back the march of socialism by softpedaling. Because the time had come, Harrap had stated, to make a stand, to do something positive.

The problem was that Harrap himself had little idea how to start a revolution. He had the rank and file members of the RBP running around in circles, all of them lashing out wildly in every direction, yet achieving very little.

Lubichek saw that with the rampant fanaticism churning around within the RBP there was the fuel to build a fire. The only thing needed was direction for him to aim that fire at. Courtesy of a lucky break, Lubichek had suddenly found himself presented with two pieces of information, totally unconnected at the time. They both came from KGB intelligence sources, and as happened often, these little snippets were pushed along the lines to various departments until someone decided to redirect them to an operative in the field. By his good fortune Boris Lubichek found both of those pieces of information on his plate at once. He digested them both, put them aside and went for a long stroll. He was based in Paris at the time and it was one of his few pleasures to be able to stroll along the banks of the Seine in the evenings. He would watch the river flowing by, gaze up at the floodlit grandeur of Notre Dame, and he would think, his mind clear and sharp. He would turn over and over inside his agile mind the facets of information that he had gained.

Sometimes it was days before any logic shone through. On other nights the soothing atmosphere of the long walks would present him with a fully formed plan in hours.

On this occasion the whole scenario fell into place quickly and smoothly. It came so easily that even Lubichek wondered whether it was all too good to be true. But after he had taken the plan apart, examined it from all angles and then rebuilt the jigsaw, he decided it was too grand a scheme to abandon. If it worked, it would be on a grand scale.

If it failed . . . but he didn't dwell on that. Lubichek knew the price of failure. A KGB operative's past successes would have little bearing on his fate after a failure. If Lubichek got it wrong, his career would be over and so, possibly, might be his life. The strange thing was that he had never considered failure before. But more than once of late he had found himself thinking about old age. It seemed odd to be considering retirement. That was something for factory workers and teachers. But a KGB agent? The thought continued to nag at him until he pushed it to the back of his mind, with images of doddering old men sitting in the sun in the grounds of a big house, all talking over old times. That had made him smile, reducing his somber thoughts to unimportant daydreams.

He had filled his mind with the matter at hand, reviewing once again the information he had been presented with. He had paced along the river slowly as he considered the first interesting item, gained from a man in the pay of the KGB in England. The man was employed in the Ministry of Defence and he had passed along details about an experimental missile system, code-named Manta, that was being produced by the Americans and the British. Both countries had contributed to development and design. The only completely American contribution was the creation of the computer system that handled missile control and instruction. This was the brainchild of an American named Phillip Harriman, one of the computer-age genius designers. He had created the programs and designed the layouts almost down to the color of the keys. No one could match his brilliance or duplicate his designs. And the whole Manta concept rested on Harriman's program. Early test firing in the United States had proved one hundred percent successful. The next step had been the manufacture of four Manta units that were to undergo practical field trials in England. Harriman would spend some months in England, supervising the trials. His wife and daughter were to remain in the States during this time.

The Manta project was classified top secret. The problem with anything designated as secret was that no matter how tight security was, or how few people were in the know, the mere fact that information existed created the possibility of that information's being passed to an unauthorized party. In this case a trusted employee, with full security clearance, had access to the Manta file, and due to his homosexual impropriety with a KGB subversive operative, he became trapped in a tangled web of blackmail over photographs and videotapes. It was standard KGB procedure yet it still worked.

Part of the information on the Manta project not only detailed the trial program but also the dates and locations of those trials. Lubichek thanked the British for their obsession with putting everything down on paper in the minutest detail. There was even a personal rundown on Phillip Harriman and his family: where he was staying while in England, and details about his family homes in the United States.

Lubichek had known from the outset that there was little to be gained from possession of construction details concerning the Manta. At the end of the day it was just another missile, and there were enough of those around already. Lubichek's interest stemmed from the fact that the missiles existed in actual fact; a real missile was a usable missile. So his plan centered on hijacking the missiles and firing them. He already had his targets pinpointed.

United States Air Force bases in England.

A hit by a Manta missile, fitted with a low-yield nuclear warhead, would wipe out a base completely, destroying highly expensive equipment and the many hundreds of American personnel stationed on the base. The effect of the strike would be manifold. As well as destroying the base chosen, the strike would greatly damage the credibility of the NATO ideal, which was the defense of Europe.

NATO was under criticism already. Many people in Europe were questioning its usefulness. There was the argument that NATO was more likely to cause war than prevent it. Debates raged throughout Europe and the United States regarding the issue. Peace protesters in England had demonstrated for years outside American bases. The Greenham Common example had been given world coverage by the press and television. Certain British organizations had been campaigning for the abolition of nuclear weapons for decades. The exploding of a nuclear device over an American base would incite the British people to riot. There would be total confusion at the seats of government. Outrage. Horror. A possible breakdown of NATO credibility. The groups in Europe that were already demanding the removal of United States bases and armed forces would be given a massive boost, and the United States would be held responsible for allowing such a thing to happen.

Lubichek wasn't concerned that nuclear explosions would affect civilian areas as well as the main targets, though he was aware that radiation, even from low-yield warheads, could spread and kill. But that was part of war. And Lubichek believed that the act of terrorism was warlike. In the end it all came down to the same thing—survival. Either you survived or your enemy did. If civilians died, that was unfortunate for them, but it was a part of life, he had thought as he absentmindedly followed a pair of lovers with his eyes.

Lubichek's plan of a strike against the American bases was no different, as far as he was concerned, from the planting of a bomb in a store or on a train. It followed the same pattern as the bombing of the headquarters of the United States peacekeeping force in Beirut back in 1983. Terrorism existed to demoralize and weaken an enemy, to render his life uncertain as to the time and place of the next attack. It was a war of nerves, of stealth, of unexpected injury and death. The Manta strike against a United States base would be just such an act.

So Lubichek had his weapons—four of them—and he intended using them all. He would choose the four largest American bases in England and wipe them off the map.

The second snippet of information that came to Lubichek concerned one Alex Manson. A captain in the United States Army, Manson had been serving in

Germany until the day he, and four men who had
served with him for years, deserted. KGB sources had
been fed information for some months that Manson
was becoming dissatisfied with his lack of advancement. He had a personality flaw that required constant
recognition to bolster his ego. It was not something the
Army felt obliged to do. Within a week or so of their
desertion Manson and his group put out the word that
their services were up for sale. Lubichek had read the
intelligence reports on Manson's previous service. He
had a good combat record and also had a way with the
men under his command—which explained why he
had taken four men with him when he went over the
wall. KGB sources had kept a close watch on Manson's movements, so when Lubichek requested the
whereabouts of the man, the information was on his
desk within the hour.

The first meeting took place in Amsterdam. Lubichek introduced himself as a representative of the
RBP. He offered Manson a long-term contract that
would pay well and would push Manson's name to the
forefront of mercenary circles. Lubichek outlined a
plan of terrorist activity, mostly fake, to see how
Manson reacted, especially when part of that plan included American military targets. Manson's response
was immediate and enthusiastic. He made it clear to
Lubichek that he no longer considered himself a
United States citizen. As far as he was concerned he
would destroy anything Lubichek pointed his finger
at.

It was not until a fortnight later, when he had witnessed Manson's expertise in planning, that Lubichek
revealed two things to the ex-captain: that he, Lubichek, was KGB, and that the plan he wanted to have

executed involved the hijacking of the secret Manta missiles. Again Manson accepted involvement, and even contributed toward the actual planning of the hijack. He helped organize RBP men for the kidnapping of Phillip Harriman.

While that was being laid out, Lubichek was in touch with a KGB contact in the United States. Through this contact Lubichek was able to deal with members of the Mafia and make a deal. It involved the kidnapping of Phillip Harriman's wife and daughter from their New Mexico ranch, according to Lubichek's instructions.

Things had rolled along well until the bungled attempt at the elimination of Jake Tasker had brought a new element into the game.

The man named McCarter.

Luckily the evacuation of the Rainham site had been well under way by the time of McCarter's escape so Lubichek kept up the momentum. Manson's handling of the RBP rank and file had been excellent, stopping any dissent before it had time to manifest.

As they rolled through the night, heading for the base, Lubichek decided that the slight setback could be accepted. Provided that the plan was concluded satisfactorily, the Rainham episode would be forgotten. As far as Lubichek was concerned it already had been forgotten.

He had far more important matters ahead of him.

Waiting for him at the base were the four nuclear devices and the Libyans who would affix them to the Mantas. The Hezbollah terrorists had been only too pleased to provide the warheads when Lubichek had told them he intended using them against American bases in England. As far as the Hezbollah were concerned, the British were associated with the Americans in any number of atrocities against Islam, and deserved the fate of their accomplices.

Lubichek glanced outside and noticed that the darkness was fading. Dawn lightened the sky. He settled back in the car seat. A new day stretched ahead of him. It was going to be a long day, but if things went the way he had planned, it could turn out to be a good day for him.

16

"How close does this get us?" Calvin James asked.

Tomas Rojhas, one of Costigan's deputies, pointed to the pile of fragments he had dug from the tire treads and suspension of the Buick. "Needles are from piñon. This here is from a juniper. See the purple berries." Picking up a mashed orange-colored flower that had been caught up in a suspension spring, he said, "Indian paintbrush."

"All this grows a few thousand feet up," Costigan explained. "On the timberline. Higher up you'd get Ponderosa pine and cedars."

"I understand," James said. "It means this car has been up in the high country."

"Quick, ain't he," Costigan said with a grin.

"The timberline must run a long way," Encizo suggested.

"*Sí,*" Rojhas agreed. "But you can still sometimes pin down a plant to a particular area."

"Can you in this case?" Encizo asked eagerly.

Rojhas was studying the crushed Indian paintbrush. He turned it over in his strong brown fingers.

"I think so," he said finally. He showed the flower to Costigan. "The east slope of the Jicarilla Ridge."

"Yeah?" Costigan examined the flower. "I think you're right, Tom."

Encizo and James waited, trying to curb their impatience.

"Jicarilla Ridge is part of the San Andres foothills about sixty miles from here," Costigan said. "Local hot spot during the Apache wars. The ridge peaks out at nine thousand feet. Along the eastern slope Indian paint grows with a flower a shade darker than anywhere else. Legend is it's got something to do with innocent blood spilled during a massacre in the 1880s. Local botanist says it has to do with natural pigmentation in the soil in that area being absorbed by the plants over the years."

Encizo nodded. "All right. We'll accept that the car has been in a particular vicinity, and perhaps it's where our kidnappers have the Harrimans. It still is a big area. Am I right?"

"Hell, yes," Costigan said.

"Hold on," James interrupted. "I think we can cut this closer. The kidnappers will need to be in contact with their accomplices. So they'll need communications. A telephone. They will also need a roof over their heads."

"There are telephone and power lines around that area," Costigan said.

"Hey!" Tomas Rojhas said. "What about the lodge?"

"What's that?"

"About four years ago a company came and built this fancy tourist lodge up on the ridge," Costigan explained. "They figured to cater for the hunters and the folk wanting a mountain vacation. Trouble was it didn't work out that way. Nobody ever came to stay. Place shut down after a year. Been closed ever since.

It just sits there now waiting on a buyer. There's a resident caretaker lives on the premises is all.''

"Could be what we're looking for," James said.

"It's worth a look," Encizo agreed.

"You fellers will be needing a ride, I figure," Costigan said, eyeing the bullet-riddled Chrysler.

"We'd be grateful, Sheriff."

"Yeah." Costigan turned to Rojhas. "Tom, stay here while the cleanup team arrives. I'm going to run Butch and Sundance here back to town. Fix 'em up with a new motor."

"Thanks for the help, Tom," James called.

"Muchos gracias," repeated Encizo.

Rojhas shrugged. *"De nada."*

James and Encizo, carrying their luggage and their weapons carryall, climbed into Costigan's patrol car. The sheriff turned the car around and headed to Trinity, away from the scene of the firefight.

An hour and a half had passed since the confrontation with the men from the Buick. The Phoenix commandos had driven the Buick up to the Harriman ranch and had telephoned Costigan from the empty house. The sheriff and his deputy had arrived shortly after James and Encizo returned to the shot-up Chrysler. Costigan had taken a long, hard look at the scene that confronted him.

"Whose toes did you step on?"

"Somebody in a touchy mood," James had said.

"Well, hell, boys, you sure did hit 'em where it hurts."

"When they come at you the way these guys did, it's the only way," James said.

Costigan had picked up one of the Uzis. "They sure enough came hunting bear."

Thanks to Rojhas, it looked as though the Phoenix pair had a possible line to the kidnappers.

But first they needed to pick up fresh transport.

"Hey," Costigan said from the front seat. "I got a chopper on the pad back in town. She was on duty when you arrived, and I never thought to mention her. But you're welcome to use her if you want."

"Thanks," James said. "It will be a faster way of getting to the lodge."

"Sheriff, can you fix us up with a map showing the location?" Encizo asked. "And maybe your pilot will know some landing place well away from the place."

"Can do," Costigan said. He jammed his foot to the floor, pushing the patrol car to its limit. As he drove, he used the radio to call ahead and gave orders for the helicopter to be made ready for a flight.

BACK AT THE SHERIFF'S OFFICE Encizo put in a call to Hal Brognola at Stony Man, giving him a rundown on their progress.

"Are you both okay?" the Fed asked.

"No sweat," Encizo said. "We got a bit dusty, but we're fine." He paused. "But the rent-a-car..."

"Yeah?" growled Brognola.

"It got a little scratched," Encizo said.

Across the room Calvin James was grinning from ear to ear at his partner's understatement.

"How *scratched*?" Brognola wanted to know.

"Well, maybe more than scratched," Encizo admitted. "Maybe it's close to being a write-off."

"You hotshots," Brognola grumbled.

"Have you had any word from the rest of the guys?" Encizo asked.

"Last I heard they had arrived. David's got himself kidnapped. And now we've got four nuclear devices smuggled into England to be fitted to the hijacked Manta units."

"What the hell are they thinking of doing with those things?"

"I wish I knew," Brognola said.

"If we can pick up any intel, we'll pass it to you," Encizo said.

"We need it," Brognola replied. "Hold on, we've got that readout from Aaron."

Aaron "the Bear" Kurtzman was Stony Man's resident computer wizard and a giant of a man, now confined to a wheelchair after the attack on Stony Man that had taken the life of April Rose, Mack Bolan's love, and pushed the Executioner out into the world on his own once more. Kurtzman had access to more files, official and unofficial, than anyone could guess. If there was information stored somewhere, Kurtzman would dig it out.

"Interesting reading," Brognola said. "Apparently the lodge is owned by a company fronting for the Mob. Aaron has managed to access files that show a direct link between Southwest Leisure Inc., the company *owning* the lodge, and Anthony Scarpetta, an East Coast mafioso."

"Makes things a little clearer," Encizo said. "The guys who hit us were East Coast types. Even the local motel owner where they stayed described them as out-of-staters."

"Keep in touch," Brognola said. "And good luck."

Encizo repeated the conversation for Calvin James.

"Sounds good," the black warrior said. "According to Costigan, the helicopter should be able to drop us as close as a couple of miles from the lodge without them hearing us."

They made a final weapons check. Encizo wore his 9 mm Smith & Wesson, with a Walther PPK for backup. He also carried his Cold Steel Tanto knife. As usual his main weapon was his Heckler & Koch MP-5 SMG. Calvin James's M-16 was loaded with a 30-round magazine. He carried his Colt Commander in a shoulder rig and also toted his G-96 knife. Both Phoenix warriors were clad in black combat gear. Belts around their waists held pouches into which were clipped extra magazines for their weapons. After a brief discussion they had decided against taking grenades. The M-33 fragmentation grenade was an effective weapon but had little discretion as to who its victims were. There was too big a risk involved with Harriman's wife and daughter to consider. At least gunfire could be selective, unlike the flying shrapnel from an exploding grenade.

"You ready?" Encizo asked.

James nodded, hefting his M-16. "Let's go and wrap this up."

17

The Red Britannia Party headquarters was in a large
run-down Victorian house standing in its own grounds
and surrounded by a brick wall. The untended gardens flanking the building were waist high with grass,
weeds and thick bushes. It was obvious that the RBP
had little time for maintaining a good image. A gravel
drive led up to the house from the wide gateway,
though the gates themselves were long gone. All that
remained were the stone pillars that had supported
them. A number of cars were parked outside the front
entrance.

Dexter had been right about the neighborhood. Di-
lapidated houses lined the litter-strewn street. There
were even a couple of abandoned cars dismally hugging the sidewalks.

The Range Rover was parked just inside the drive-
way of an empty house. Two more houses stood between Phoenix Force and the RBP headquarters. The
sky was just beginning to show the first hints of light,
and a certain mellowness to the air promised a warm
day. The force was geared up for the assault because
they had made extensive preparations....

ON THEIR RETURN to the safehouse from Rainham,
Katz had insisted that McCarter receive medical at-

tention. Dexter had made arrangements quickly. The medic had turned out to be a young woman with a no-nonsense attitude, and it appeared that even McCarter wouldn't be able to resist her particular brand of common sense. She ordered him into a side room, closing the door firmly.

While that was happening, Katz made a telephone call to Hal Brognola. He wanted to give the Fed an update on the situation and ask if Aaron Kurtzman could come up with any information on the names McCarter had learned during his time as a prisoner of the RBP.

Dexter went off to arrange for food and coffee, leaving Manning and Hahn to ready the equipment Phoenix Force would need for the raid on the RBP headquarters. Katz had decided they would go in hard. The knowledge that the RBP was in possession of nuclear devices had lent a sense of urgency that demanded swift and relentless effort. Time was running out. Phoenix Force *had* to locate the secret base where the Manta missiles were, and they had to do it quickly.

Manning and Hahn laid out combat blacksuits. They took out a box containing flash-bang concussion grenades. Ammunition for the force's weapons was loaded into empty magazines.

When McCarter emerged from the examination room thirty minutes later, he had a dressing on his shoulder and a smug expression on his face. The doctor, following him closely, seemed to have lost some of her profession composure.

"How is he, Doc?" Gary Manning asked.

"He's, er...fine," she replied. "But he really should rest. I've put stitches in that shoulder wound and given him an injection. The bruises and facial injuries will be sore for a while but they'll heal.''

"No permanent damage?" Manning asked.

"He'll live."

"Of course I will, love," McCarter said. "And all due to your tender healing touch."

"Thanks, Doc," Manning said. "Don't mind his chatter. It's a family failing."

She smiled and glanced briefly at McCarter, who gave her a big wink. "Thanks, Doc," he said. "If I have a relapse, I'll send for you."

As the door closed behind her, Manning glanced at McCarter. The British Phoenix pro was getting into his combat gear.

"Just what did you get up to in there?"

McCarter managed to look offended. He shoved one leg into his blacksuit. "You know I'm not supposed to disclose what takes place between doctor and patient," he said.

"Surely that's the doctor's line?" Hahn pointed out.

"Is it?" McCarter asked innocently, then allowed an indulgent smirk to spread on his face.

"Are you sure those RBP goons didn't whack you on the head?" Manning asked, but McCarter didn't answer and carried on dressing, humming softly to himself until the door opened to admit Katz.

"'The Bear' came through for us," he said. "Manson is Alex Manson, U.S. Army deserter. He quit without notice a couple of months back along with four others from his unit—men who have served with him for years. Within his limitations Manson was a good soldier. His profile describes him as having something of a personality hang-up. It's what stopped him getting a higher rank than captain, even though he served in Nam and achieved a good combat record."

"What about our little Russkie chum?" McCarter asked.

"Boris Lubichek. KGB. Mid-forties. Something of a mystery man. The stories going around say he's good. For a KGB operative he seems to have a lot of freedom when it comes to decision making."

"I'll make some decisions for him if I get my hands on the blighter," McCarter threatened.

"Hey, you know what your doctor said," Manning interrupted. "Take it easy."

"Up yours," McCarter replied rudely.

"I think he's getting better," Hahn remarked.

"You mean back to his usual obnoxious self?" Manning asked.

Katz held up his hand. "Quiet, you two, I haven't finished yet. Hal said he's heard from Rafael and Calvin. They made contact with the kidnappers and took a number of them out in a firefight. It appears they may have located where Harriman's family is being held. That's their next move."

"No problem, then," McCarter said without looking up. "Don't know why we worry."

"Right now all we have to worry about is getting inside the RBP headquarters," Katz pointed out. "Let's get our gear together. Then we can eat and get a couple of hours' rest. We'll hit the RBP site at dawn."

Katz's SIG-Sauer P-226 was the first of the Israeli's weapons to be loaded and checked, followed by his backup gun, a .380 Beretta he carried in a pancake holster against the small of his back. Katz expertly examined his 9 mm Uzi SMG before he clicked home a thirty-two round magazine.

The careful attention paid to weapons was extremely worthwhile. The middle of a firefight was no place to find a weapon seizing up due to neglect, and experience had demonstrated that no gun could be expected to work perfectly if it was not serviced. When a man was in combat, there had to be only one thought in his mind—the fight itself. If he was worrying about his weapon functioning, he had no right being involved in the battle to start with. Not only would he be putting his own life at risk but also the lives of his companions. That was something that would never happen with Phoenix Force. A Phoenix Force member would never contemplate such a selfish act as risking the lives of others because of his negligence. It was why the team had been so successful. They thought and acted as one. In combat their actions were coordinated and it was that unity that won through each time.

Such thoughts may have been in Gary Manning's mind as he laid out and checked his weapons. Although the Canadian was the team's sharpshooter and normally carried a high-powered rifle, scoped for long-distance sniping, his current choice was a 9 mm Uzi. The raid on the RBP house was going to be close quarters combat, so the adaptable Phoenix pro selected a tool for the task. He did not change, or even think of changing his handgun. Manning's .357 Magnum Desert Eagle was the only weapon he would consider. The powerful autoloader, with its 158-grain wadcutters, was a superb creation. The Israeli pistol had high accuracy coupled with low recoil; it was a man stopper that packed a terrific punch.

Karl Hahn, likewise, would have resented anyone's trying to make him change from his Heckler & Koch MP-5. The 9 mm SMG was one of the most accurate of its kind. It had single-shot or automatic fire, even a 3-round burst facility, and with its eight hundred rounds per minute cyclic rate of fire it dealt out death in the winking of an eye. The German ace had similar feelings about his Walther P-5. As far as he was concerned, it was the best handgun around. It had pulled him out of many tight corners and would do so again.

The irascible David McCarter liked nothing better than to get into a heated argument about weapons. It gave him the opportunity of sounding off about his personal choice. His 9 mm M-10 Ingram was almost an extension of the ex-SAS operative's hands. The Briton also swore by his Browning Hi-Power 9 mm pistol, but to be on the safe side, he did carry a backup weapon in the shape of a Charter Arms .38 Special.

The Phoenix team went about their weapons drill with practiced ease until they were satisfied. The arms were given a final check, loaded, then laid in readiness while the super commandos refreshed themselves with the food and drink provided by Dexter.

DAWN WAS MAKING serious inroads into the night with a pearly glow, and with the objective in sight, Phoenix Force was set to go.

"Do you think they will be expecting us?" Karl Hahn asked.

"I'm bloody certain they will," McCarter replied. "Somebody at the Rainham base will have tipped them off."

"So maybe this bunch has pulled out as well," Manning said.

"Maybe I'm a horse's ass!" McCarter muttered, anxious to get into action. "Let's go and find out."

"One thing," Katz reminded them. "Our main aim is to gather information. We need to know where the missiles are being kept. If we get in a firefight you shouldn't take risks just to keep someone alive—but remember our objective."

"Do you want me in on this?" Dexter asked.

Katz shook his head. "No offence, Dexter," he said, "but we function better as a team. Knowing one another means we don't have to worry whether the next man is doing his job. We're more than grateful for the way you've ferried us round since we arrived. It's saved us valuable time."

Dexter accepted the Israeli's reasoning.

"On second thoughts there is something you could do," Katz said suddenly. "Wait until we go in. As soon as you hear gunfire, that'll be your signal to block the gateway with the Rover. Just in case any of them make a run for it."

"All right," Dexter agreed.

"You armed?" Manning asked.

"Handgun." Dexter showed his holstered Browning Hi-Power.

"Sensible chap," McCarter said when he spotted it. He reached into the back of the Range Rover and lifted a spare Uzi from the weapons bag.

"Have you handled one of those before?" Katz asked.

Dexter took the Uzi. He inserted the magazine McCarter handed him, cocked the weapon and laid it across his lap.

"I'll manage," he said.

Phoenix Force exited the Range Rover, gathering around Katz. "We can approach the house by using the neighboring gardens," the Israeli commando said. "When we go over the last wall we'll split. Gary and I will make a frontal assault. David, you team with Karl and take the rear. Let's synchronize watches. I have 6:12. We'll give ourselves ten minutes to get in position. We go in at 6:22. *Try* for prisoners."

The others nodded, then they all melted into the undergrowth and vanished from sight.

Dexter watched them go from his seat in the Range Rover. He started the motor and allowed it to tick over. Then he settled down to wait.

18

Dropping over the high brick wall, the Phoenix warriors and their ally crouched in the thick bushes. They had reached the garden of the RBP headquarters without being seen.

"Hey, somebody is home," Manning whispered, indicating an upstairs window. A man stood behind the dusty glass, drinking from a thick mug.

McCarter nudged Hahn on the arm. "Come on, Karl." The pair slipped away, working along the base of the wall toward the rear of the rambling old house.

Katz and Manning approached the front of the house through the heavy undergrowth. They worked their way past the parked cars, then scuttled across the exposed stretch of drive until they were pressed hard up against the front wall of the house, only feet away from the double front doors.

Katz took a look at his watch. They had reached the house with almost a minute to spare.

As they waited for the seconds to tick away, each of the Phoenix warriors took out a concussion grenade, popped the pin and held the grenade ready.

Glancing again at his watch, Katz saw they had ten seconds left. He began to count them off in a whisper just loud enough for Manning to hear. Three... two... one... zero!

"Go!" he said.

The Canadian tough guy took off and hit the front doors with his hard shoulder, bursting them wide open. Katz had followed close behind. As the doors were smashed back on their hinges, he and Manning lobbed their stun grenades into the building, then ducked aside.

A startled yell from inside the house was punctuated by the crack of the grenades. There was also a blinding flash of light and a billowing cloud of smoke, followed seconds later by similar explosions erupting at the rear of the RBP headquarters.

Hard in the wake of the explosions, Katz and Manning burst through the open front doors into wreaths of white smoke swirling across the entrance hall. The Phoenix pair split as they breached the entrance, Katz taking the left side, Manning the right.

A dazed figure was crawling on hands and knees across the hall, blood trickling from one ear. Farther away a second man leaned against a wall, his hands clamped tightly over his ears.

Movement at the head of the stairs on Gary Manning's side of the hall caught his eye. He flattened himself against the wall, tracking the vague shadow with his Uzi.

An RBP fanatic suddenly darted down the stairs, revealing the stubby Interdynamic Mini 99 held close to his side. As the muzzle came up, the trigger was pulled. A hot stream of 9 mm parabellum slugs cut through the air and finally blasted ragged holes in the wall. He hadn't allowed for the fact that he was descending the stairs.

Gary Manning did not make the same elementary mistake. His Uzi was on target when he pulled the trigger, sending a volley into the fanatic's chest. The slugs penetrated the chest wall, and the force of the hits spun the man off his feet and against the wall. Coughing blood, the dying gunman cartwheeled the rest of the way to the bottom of the stairs.

A trio of yelling men burst from a door at the far end of the hall. They were all armed, and just like the opposition McCarter had tangled with, proved that it takes more than just being able to hold a deadly weapon to be effective with it. Two of them carried Uzis, and the third had an Ingram. They were spraying bullets in all directions as though they were eligible for a bonus for most shots fired. Slugs plowed into the wall and chewed ragged splinters out of the floorboards.

Yakov Katzenelenbogen calmly sighted along his Uzi and sent a well-directed burst in the direction of the approaching trio, who dashed straight into the hail of bullets. The first let out a howl and threw his arms into the air as if in supplication. But he was bleeding to death rapidly, and before he had even fallen to the floor, the guy next to him stopped a hail of slugs with his hip. The man was spun off his feet and fell directly into a blast from Manning's gun as the Canadian turned to assist Katz. The last of the trio was caught in a cross fire of Phoenix guns, and his torso seemed to disintegrate under the violent merging of two streams of hot lead. For a moment he was obscured by a fine spray of blood, then his remains hit the floor.

Katz turned to Manning. "Cover me," he yelled above the rattle of gunfire coming from the rear of the house.

He darted forward and crouched beside the man he'd first spotted when he entered the house. The man hadn't yet regained his balance due to the effect of the stun grenade and was still on his knees. Katz slugged him with the barrel of his Uzi, flattening the RBP goon to the floor. Reaching into the pocket of his combat suit, Katz pulled out plastic riot handcuffs. He looped one over the ankles and pulled them together, then he pulled the limp arms together and slipped a second plastic loop over the wrists.

The gunfire had advanced from the back parts of the house and was accompanied by the sound of yelling and pounding footsteps. His prisoner secured, Katz snatched up his Uzi and turned to face a gunman wielding an automatic pistol. The RBP goon fired first, but his bullet zipped by Katz's face. Katz dropped to a crouch, and squeezed off a burst at the RBP guy's angry face. His 9 mm burst was short, and to the point. There would be no more quarrels for them to settle. As his foe's face disintegrated before his eyes, Katz loosed a stream of 9 mm messengers of final release and ended his agony.

Manning had heard pounding footsteps above him and darted toward the stairs, anticipating the appearance of more RBP gunmen. He was right. As the Canadian powerhouse hit the lower stairs, three of the enemy burst into view on the upper landing.

Only the first of the three even managed to get off a shot, and that went into the wall above Manning's head. Immediately the Phoenix pro opened up with his Uzi. A stream of 9 mm sizzlers splintered the banister rails in front of the three RBP men. The air was filled with exploding wood that flew into the faces of the trio. One of them staggered back with a six-inch dagger of wood embedded in his neck. As he stumbled away from the banister, he grabbed the splinter and tore it from his neck, not realizing that he had ripped open his carotid artery. That only dawned on him when blood began to pump out of the ragged wound. Panic set in, and he began to thrash around, unwittingly increasing the flow of his lifeblood. He died squirming around on the floor in a slippery pool of his own blood.

Death came to the remaining pair somewhat more swiftly. Although cut by the flying splinters, they were able to continue functioning for a few seconds longer. That was possible because Manning's Uzi had clicked empty. Aware that the remaining two men might return fire at any second, the Canadian ace held the Uzi in his left hand, while his right unleathered his Desert Eagle. The powerful .357 man stopper tracked in on the closest of the two and slammed out its shots with precision. A pair of bone crushers cored through the fanatic's skull, and the impact tossed him across the landing in a loose heap. The last man in the group barely had time to register what had happened to his companions before his own world exploded in his face. The first .357 round struck directly below his nose, its upward trajectory guiding it up into his skull where it burned through his brain. Manning's follow-up bullet, though superfluous, ripped in through the guy's neck and exited by the back of his head. He flopped down across the banister rail, hung there for a moment, then fell. The sound of his landing was drowned by the continuing gunfire.

Katz, reloading his Uzi, caught Manning's eye. "We'll work our way through to join up with David and Karl," he said.

"Okay," Manning called. He retreated from the stairs, holstering his Desert Eagle. Ejecting the empty magazine, he slipped a fresh one into the Uzi and cocked it. "I'll cover our backs in case there are any more up there still in a fighting mood."

"At least we have one alive," the Phoenix commander said, indicating the RBP man he had secured. "Let's see if David manages to leave somebody alive."

THE STUN GRENADES DELIVERED by McCarter and Hahn went in through the windows of the house's large kitchen. Seconds after the loud explosions, McCarter booted open the kitchen door. Hahn let go with a blast from his MP-5 to cover McCarter, who went in low through the open door, diving to the right. Hahn followed close on his heels, taking the left.

The kitchen had a lone occupant. Despite the severe and painful concussion received from the exploding grenades, the terrorist came out fighting. He had a .45-caliber Colt Commander in his hand as he staggered to his feet from behind the long kitchen table, and he opened fire. Bullets sizzled through the air, clanging off kitchen utensils and howling off the walls. It was obvious that the still bedazzled man was firing from instinct.

Karl Hahn had no desire to stop one of the .45-caliber projectiles. Down on one knee, he angled the muzzle of his MP-5 up at the RBP terrorist and put a stop to the wild shooting. But there was nothing wild or reckless about the German's aim. A single, stunned cry burst from the enemy's lips as his heart and lungs were torn by the angry slugs. Blood erupted from his mangled flesh as he did an ungraceful back flip and hit the stone floor of the kitchen.

"One down," McCarter observed as he kicked open the door leading through to the main part of the house. A long, wide passage lay ahead, and some distance from them a narrow flight of stairs led to the upper floors.

Almost the same instant that McCarter and Hahn burst out from the kitchen, a door swung open at the far end of the passage and armed men swept through.

"They look an ugly crowd," McCarter growled just as the RBP terrorists opened fire. The passage became a shooting gallery, with the Phoenix commando twosome the targets. But it was the kind of shooting gallery where the targets shot back, and being Phoenix warriors, they returned fire with pinpoint accuracy.

McCarter swept the passage with his favorite Ingram. The Briton's M-10 crackled fiercely, and scorching bullets tore into the lead RBP men to eliminate them from the next bout. They went down in a bloody haze as McCarter's blast knocked their legs from under them.

Flattened against the wall of the hallway, Karl Hahn turned his Heckler & Koch subgun in the direction of the terrorists and hosed them with its deadly fire. He was rewarded with the sight of three fanatics tossed aside by the raking stream of deadly 9 mm parabellums.

Seeing a number of their companions going down so quickly caused the rest of the RBP bunch to hesitate. It was a fatal mistake because David McCarter spotted their indecision and took advantage of it with exact instincts and precision. With a wild yell the

Phoenix warrior raced down the passage, opening up with his Ingram.

The sight of the approaching black-clad commando unnerved the opposition and removed any initiative for strategy or regrouping. They quickly began to understand the reality of their chosen calling was far removed from the rosy picture Alex Manson had painted for them. They were supposed to do the killing, but despite the gleaming, deadly weapons they had been given, death had turned against them, his clawing hand already claiming a harvest of corpses. Only they were RBP corpses, not their enemy.

McCarter, if he had been able to read the terrorist's minds, would have done nothing to allay their fears. He had seen the stunned looks on their faces, and realizing they were starting to panic had seized the advantage.

Jammed in the doorway, each trying to get past the other, the RBP hoodlums were trapped. In the end they died without returning McCarter's fire, their bodies becoming bloody rags.

As the Briton reloaded his Ingram, Hahn advanced beyond the dead terrorists, through the door leading to a long room that had once been an elegant dining room but was now used as temporary barracks. Rows of low army cots lined the floor, and the room stank of sweat and beer. Empty cans were scattered about the place, along with crumpled food packages. In a corner a coffee percolator bubbled away. A television set displayed an early-morning news program in silence.

There was a shadow of movement at the far end of the room. Hahn saw the barrel of the gun edged around the door, then an unshaved angry face appeared. Hahn and the terrorist locked eyes in the same instant, then the man lunged out from behind the door, firing as he moved. Hahn remained where he was as he touched his trigger.

The terrorist's bullets burned the air over Hahn's left shoulder, one clipping the fabric of the German warrior's combat suit. But time was running out for a repeat performance as a stream of 9 mms punched into the RBP fanatic's chest with enough force to pick him up and ram him bodily into the wall at his back. He died coughing and wondering briefly what had gone wrong and why it was happening to him. The situation didn't favor deep thought, though, and he died before he could figure out the answer.

While Hahn was dealing with the terrorist in the room ahead of him, McCarter was reloading his Ingram. In the momentary calm after Hahn had dispatched his terrorist, McCarter's ears picked up a faint sound behind him. It was no more than the softest creak of wood when weight is placed on it. Like a foot being cautiously lowered onto a wooden stair tread.

As he thought of the stairs behind him, and slightly to the left, McCarter reacted instinctively. He knew he had little chance of completing his reload of the Ingram. So he forgot about the subgun, letting it slip from his fingers and allowing his body to drift to the left, bending his knees as he sank to the floor. His right hand reached up for the holstered Browning Hi-Power, fingers gripping the butt.

A gun roared from somewhere overhead. The bullet whacked the floor hard by his heel.

McCarter carried on with his evasive movements, going straight into a fall that he cushioned with his left hand, then continued on into a shoulder roll, twisting his body as he came into contact with the floor. His right hand, gripping the Hi-Power, reached across his own body, seeking its target, and as McCarter's eyes fixed the position of the man on the stairs, he triggered two quick shots. The first ripped into the target's left shoulder, dropping him back against the stairs. McCarter's second slug caused another serious, though not life-threatening injury. McCarter might have let him go on living if he had quit there and then, but the wounded terrorist burned a couple more bullets in McCarter's direction. One thudded into the wall near McCarter's head and exploded a shower of splintered brick against the Briton's face. The sting of the splinters triggered an instinctive and sharp reaction. His Browning spit twice more, sending a pair of death dealers that didn't allow for any argument.

McCarter climbed to his feet, picking up his discarded Ingram. He finished loading it, then glanced briefly at the dead man on the stairs before rejoining Hahn. Although he didn't know it, the corpse with the bullet-mangled face was Alex Manson's ex-sergeant, Ron Kovic.

Katz and Manning were moving toward the rear of the house when they heard a few straggling shots coming from there, then heavy silence descended.

Pausing at one side of an open door, Katz held his Uzi at the ready.

"David? Karl?" he called.

"Ho!" came Karl Hahn's reply.

Moments later the four warriors were reunited.

"Do you think there could be more?" Hahn asked.

"If there are, they're staying low," Manning said.

"Like it or not," Katz told them, "we'll have to do a room-to-room. We can't take a chance of overlooking even one."

"This is the bit I hate," McCarter grumbled. "Why can't they come out and fight? Bugger this poking around in corners. It's like being a bloody rat catcher."

"It's rats we're after," Katz pointed out. "Two-legged ones called terrorists."

McCarter sighed in resignation. "All right," he relented. "Let's get on with it. There's nothing else exciting happening around here."

He was right. Nothing did happen as they combed the now silent house. The long, fruitless search revealed that there were no more RBP terrorists in the place. Phoenix Force quit the headquarters with their live captive in tow and returned to the safehouse for a full assessment of their next steps.

19

The hour had come. It was a clear, starlit night. The mountain air was cool, tangy with the scent of pine.

In concealment behind the thick stand of pines edging the wide parking area that fronted the lodge, Rafael Encizo and Calvin James were silently taking stock of the situation to judge the lay of the land.

It was just after midnight.

The lodge lay immediately before them, resting on the low bluff that jutted out from the timbered mountain slopes. Constructed from local lumber and stone, the lodge's modern lines blended unobtrusively with the surroundings and didn't take away from the impact of the natural setting. A clean, stylish building with big expanses of glass, the lodge could easily have housed a large number of guests.

But the Phoenix duo knew it wasn't guests they might have to deal with. Their business was decidedly serious. The kind that could easily end in violent conflict.

For the sake of the kidnapped wife and daughter of Phillip Harriman, Encizo and James were hoping that—given the advantage of surprise—they could carry off their penetration of the lodge with relative ease, and especially, with controlled use of firepower. It was all too easy for a firefight to suck in innocent victims. With that in mind Encizo and James were going to try to effect a low-level entry.

One of their problems was that they did not know how many of the enemy they would have to contend with. According to the intel they had gained, previously there had been six. If they discounted the four killed during the desert firefight, that should have left two.

But outside the lodge were parked three almost identical cars plus a battered 4×4 that probably belonged to the caretaker.

"Either that caretaker is a car buff," James said, "or he's got family visiting."

"They may be *family*," Encizo agreed. "But not his."

"Damn!" James exclaimed. "That heightens the risk of the Harrimans' getting injured. It's not as simple as we'd hoped."

"Is it ever?" his Cuban partner asked.

"There could be another half dozen in there," James pointed out. "Or more."

"We'll handle it," Encizo said.

Calvin James nodded, accepting the situation as it was. Phoenix Force always rose to the challenge, no matter what the odds, never opting for the easy way out. It was the way they operated. When the force accepted a mission, they also accepted the hazards coming with it. It made life a permanent risk, but none of them would have had it any other way.

"You spotted any guards yet?" James asked.

Encizo shook his head.

They had patrolled the periphery of the lodge for the past half hour in ever-narrowing circles to establish whether there were any lookouts. So far their efforts hadn't turned up anything, and their beat had brought them to the spot overlooking the parking area and the lodge frontage.

Encizo nudged James and with a nod indicated in which direction to train his gaze, then pointed at a figure that had detached itself from the deep shadows at the bottom of the sloping drive that led to the building's main entrance. As the figure moved into a patch of moonlight, the Phoenix pair saw that it was a man carrying a stubby SMG.

James put down his M-16 soundlessly and drew out his G-96 knife. Silently he showed Encizo the weapon, then jerking his head in the man's direction, said, "Let's get this one alive. He could give us some info on who's inside."

Encizo took up a position where he could watch the surrounding area and provide cover for James. No words had passed between them regarding the tactic because they were well tuned to each other's operational techniques within the team. The survival of the force as a whole depended on the smooth cooperation and functioning of its individual members.

The deep velvet shadows of the forest enfolded Calvin James as he inched his way to a position close to the wandering path of the guard. He measured and weighed each step to move as soundlessly as possible through the scrub beneath the pines. He created barely a sound and moved as one with the night.

Reaching the edge of the parking area, James stopped and knelt at the base of a thick pine. He waited, and a slight breeze whispered through the trees, rearranging the shadows for a minute. But the black ex-SWAT member was well versed in the practice of concealment and stealth. His stint with the special operations group in Vietnam had provided him with on-the-spot experience that was never to be forgotten. And James was relying on those skills tonight.

The guard came into view again. He wandered casually along his route. His silenced Ingram MAC-10 was cradled in his arm, and a long, thin cigar glowed in his free hand, its aromatic smoke drifting to reach James's nostrils. It was obvious the man's mind was on other things.

James let the guard go past his position. As he walked on, James rose from the darkness like a phantom. Two long strides, and he was directly behind his target. He lashed out with his right foot, catching the guard's left leg at the back of the knee. As he uttered a choked grunt, the man's numbed leg buckled and threw him off balance. Even as he sagged to the ground, James lunged forward, driving the edge of his left hand across the back of the exposed neck. The guard went down, hitting the ground hard and reflexively letting the Ingram spill from his fingers. James followed him down, slamming a knee into his lower back. Grabbing a handful of thick, oiled hair, he yanked the man's head back until the muscles in his neck bulged under the strain. Then he laid the razorsharp edge of the G-96 against the taut neck, applying just enough pressure to break the skin and allow a thin trickle of blood to escape.

"Talk to me," James said in a harsh stage whisper. He tightened his hold just in case the stunned guard didn't get the point, then continued. "Have the Harrimans been harmed?"

"No!" the guard choked out, anxious to talk. James had convinced him he could die quickly if he didn't cooperate. "They ain't been touched, just shook around some." The cold knife blade pressed a little harder, cut a little deeper. "Jesus Christ, what can I say?"

"Any more like you wandering around outside?" James asked as he pressed the blade harder, making it nick a little deeper.

"No."

"How long before you finish your stretch?"

"Couple hours."

"How many in the lodge?"

"Five inside. That's it, I swear."

"The Harrimans?"

"Second floor. Room 12."

"Anybody with them?"

"Just one guy."

James let go of the guard's hair. As Encizo came up and covered the man with his weapon, James fished a pair of plastic riot cuffs from his pocket. "Hands together, behind your back," he ordered, and when the guard obeyed James slipped the cuffs over his wrists and pulled them tight, then repeated the operation on his ankles.

James took the M-16 Encizo handed him. There was a length of black adhesive tape stuck lightly to the stock. After removing the tape, James plastered it over the guard's mouth. Then the two Phoenix warriors took hold of the guard's leather belt and dragged the bound man into the cover of the trees.

"Did we get anything?" Encizo asked.

James nodded affirmatively and repeated the guard's information for Encizo's benefit.

"All right," the Cuban said. "What's our plan?"

"Our main concern is getting Harriman's wife and daughter out safely," James said.

"First we have to reach them."

"Knowing where they are will make it easier," James pointed out.

"Calvin, you ought to know by now that nothing in this game ever comes easy," Encizo said, and as if to confirm his observation, there was a shout from somewhere near the lodge.

"Vince! Hey, Vince, where the hell are you?"

Encizo prodded the bound guard. "You Vince?"

The gagged man nodded, and his captors exchanged a quick look. Then James bent to yank him into a sitting position and peel off the tape covering his mouth. The G-96 appeared in James's hand again, and he held it so the guard could see it.

"Remember this?"

The man nodded.

"Well, it still works," James promised. "Now call him over here."

The man named Vince nodded, his eyes fixed fearfully on the G-96's blade. "Over here, Augie!" he yelled.

"What's goin' on?" Augie shouted back and became visible as he crossed the parking area, heading in the direction of the voice.

"Come look what I found," Vince said loudly with an anxious glance at the knife.

The man called Augie blundered into the tangled undergrowth, cursing as it snagged his expensive clothing. "Where the hell are you, Vince?" he grumbled.

"Try here," Encizo said softly as he stepped out of the shadows at Augie's side.

Augie's head snapped around. He had realized that the voice did not belong to Vince. His right hand reached for the automatic pistol resting in his shoulder rig.

The heavy weight of Encizo's Heckler & Koch slammed across the hoodlum's jaw, spinning him off balance. Encizo followed up with a second blow to the skull, pitching him to the ground. Bending over the unconscious man, Encizo quickly cuffed and gagged him, then relieved the kidnapper of his handgun.

"Two down, four to go," James said.

"They could miss Augie any minute," Encizo pointed out. "I think it's time to go in fast."

James nodded in agreement. The appearance of the man named Augie had wiped out any opportunity of a protracted entry. Time was running out.

"All right," Encizo said, and with that they sprinted across the exposed parking area and flattened themselves against the base of the slope below the lodge.

"Go," Encizo said. "I'll cover."

James took off, darting up the curving drive. He crouched in the shadow below one of the panoramic windows fronting the building. In a little while he raised his arm and signaled. Seconds later Encizo's dark figure raced up the drive. He knelt beside James.

"Main doors are open," James said, indicating the subdued light spilling from the entrance.

"Let's hit it through the front door, then," Encizo replied.

Together they rose and ran for the half-open glass doors. They reached them at the same moment, their hands shoving the heavy, balanced doors wide open. The spacious reception hall curved away ahead of them. Comfortable chairs and couches were arranged around a central area, and beyond was the long registration counter. Only a few lights were on, throwing soft illumination over the polished wood floor. To their left a wide staircase allowed access to the upper floors.

James, pausing in the middle of the reception area, waved an arm in the direction of the staircase.

"I've got it," Encizo acknowledged, racing for the stairs.

"What's goin' on?" a heavy voice demanded.

James turned in the direction of the voice and saw a burly, unshaved man lurching into the reception area through an archway. A sign above the archway proclaimed that he'd just come from the cocktail lounge. In one hand the big man held a can of beer and in the other a .45-caliber Colt Automatic pistol.

The big man was fast for his size, and smart. His initial glance took in James, his combat gear and weaponry, then switched to Encizo, who was similarly outfitted. It didn't look as though these uninvited guests had come for the mountain air. The way they were dressed and armed meant only one thing: they were hostile, and they could only be at the lodge for one reason. To free the Harrimans!

With the speed of lighting it occurred to him these men had something to do with the fact that the others hadn't shown up or contacted the lodge. He somehow knew they had.

It was likely that Chuck and the boys were dead.

"Goddamn it, you—" he yelled, interrupting himself to swing the muzzle of the big .45 and trigger a shot at Encizo. The powerful slug whacked into the riser just behind Encizo but the Cuban kept on taking the stairs two and three at a time.

James had reacted instantaneously to the big man's sudden move. He pulled the muzzle of the M-16 into line and punched a 3-round burst into the ample body. The trio of sizzlers all hit within a tight circle, plowing deep into the chest, destroying bone and muscle. Cleaving through the internal organs, they sheared the spine as they blasted their way out the big man's back. The man took a half dozen uncoordinated steps backward, then lost control and crashed to the floor. He lay bleeding profusely, and briefly the heel of his shoe drummed against the floor.

And then there were three, James reminded himself, looking up to see Encizo vanish from sight at the top of the stairs.

An SMG opened up with a deafening racket, and 9 mm slugs hummed over Calvin James's shoulder to become embedded in the wall behind him. James, who valued his life greatly, hit the floor in a running dive. He slid across the highly polished, smooth floorboards and scrambled behind the registration desk, with bullets chopping up the wood in his wake. The desk area was riddled with a swarm of hot lead, filling the air with splinters of wood.

When the shooting subsided, James, who had eased himself to the extreme end of the long counter, peered around its base. He could see across the reception area. On the far side double doors gave access to one of the lodge's restaurants. Though he couldn't see any movement inside the darkened room, the black Phoenix commando did spot a number of shiny shell cases littering the floor just inside the doors.

That was where his attacker had fired from, and he had to be in there still. There hadn't been time for anyone to exit the room and cross the wide expanse of the reception area.

James eased his M-16 into firing position. He took quick aim, then began firing, loosing off 3-round bursts. After each burst he moved the muzzle a few inches, saturating the pair of half-open doors with a raking volley of 5.56 projectiles.

The glass and wood doors exploded under the impact. Shredded pine and fragmented glass flew in all directions as the hail of gunfire powered through them. James kept it up until he had exhausted the M-16's magazine.

Glass was still tinkling to the floor when a deep groan came from the darkened room. A shadowy figure stumbled into view, hunched over and clutching frantic hands over his injuries. Blood issued from a number of severe wounds in the kidnapper's chest and torso. Shards of broken glass and pale wood splinters stuck from his clothing and flesh like so many needles. Stumbling, he fell against the shattered frame of one of the restaurant doors. Throwing out a bloodied hand to support himself, he shoved it through one of the remaining intact glass panels. He was just in his last throes when James's M-16, now reloaded, stuttered in triplicate to send the last mercy shots.

Stepping out from behind the registration desk, Calvin James paused in midstride. The sound of gunfire from the upper floor of the lodge reached his ears. He could differentiate two types of weapons. One was a shotgun, the other an SMG—but it wasn't Encizo's H&K MP-5.

The black Phoenix warrior hit the stairs on the run. His M-16 was up and ready as he raced to help his Cuban partner.

The heavy boom of the shotgun sounded again. It was followed by a sound James was thankful to hear: the rapid crackle of Encizo's H&K MP-5.

Reaching the second floor, James caught sight of a printed sign on the wall indicating in which direction certain rooms lay. He absorbed the information even as he dashed past. At the intersection of the passage he turned left, then flattened himself against the wall as a figure in a tan suit loomed before him.

It was the man toting the shotgun, an SPAS-12. An ugly brute of a weapon, the SPAS was capable of being used either as a pump action or an autoloader. It had a nine-round magazine of twelve-gauge shells and could deliver them with deadly accuracy. With its metal parts parkerized in mat black, the Franchi SPAS combat shotgun both looked and acted the part.

James's swift evasive move only managed to take him away from the SPAS's black muzzle a fraction of a second before the gunner pulled the trigger and sent a howling charge of twelve-gauge flesh pulpers along the passage, the heat of the discharge fanning the commando's face.

Anger clouded the shotgunner's face when he saw he had missed. He stepped back, arcing the SPAS round to track in on James again, but the Phoenix hell-raiser had moved. He lashed out with his right foot, the toe of his boot landing squarely between the shotgunner's legs. The guy let out a shriek of agony as red-hot pain flared through his body, but James didn't allow him time to dwell on it. He followed through with a heavy butt stroke from his M-16, making the man go crashing against the wall. James dispatched another blow using the end of the M-16's stock. It hammered into the man's neck, crushing the windpipe. The shotgunner sagged to the floor, his life slipping from him as he lay choking in his own blood.

James scooped up the SPAS, slinging it over his shoulder as he moved on along the passage. An intersection appeared again. A few feet to the left was a window. The main passage, a long one with a number of doors leading off to bedrooms, veered to the right.

As James rounded the corner, gunfire exploded. Bullets zinged heavily through the air, chopping into the walls.

Encizo was down on the carpeted floor, returning fire. His opponent was just out of sight inside one of the bedrooms. The door stood ajar. The frame was chewed to splinters by the slugs from Encizo's H&K.

James saw his partner's problem within moments. Although Encizo had the man pinned in the room, he couldn't reach him because the kidnapper had the wall to protect him, and the 9 mms the Cuban was firing didn't have the power to penetrate.

Leaning his M-16 against the passage wall, James slipped the SPAS from his shoulder. Aiming in the direction of the doorframe, he unleashed the twelve-gauge power of the shotgun. The blast tore a chunk out of the frame and the edge of the wall. James fired again and again. Each powerful blast ripped away another shower of plaster and cinder block.

Encizo had thrown a glance over his shoulder at the first blast from the SPAS. Seeing that it was James, the Cuban had taken his cue, and as the barrage on the wall continued, Encizo crawled on his belly until he was up to the door. He laid down his MP-5 and unleathered his Smith & Wesson automatic. Drawing his knees under his body, Encizo braced himself, then launched himself forward through the door and into the room.

He landed on his left shoulder, rolling and twisting in the same movement. The completion of his roll had him facing back toward the door he had just entered.

With a desperate growl the kidnapper was already turning in Encizo's direction, bringing his Uzi to bear. The left side of the man's face was streaming blood from a dozen gashes caused by flying splinters torn from the edge of the wall by the shotgun blasts.

Encizo was in no mood for giving anyone an even break, and he simply extended his S&W, held two-handed, pulling the trigger as fast as he was able. A stream of flesh shredders punched into the kidnapper's chest and neck, slamming him back against the wall with enough force to crack the plaster. He hung there for a few seconds, then simply collapsed as his body quit functioning. As the dying gunman hit the floor, blood began to seep from the ragged holes in his body, and a thick gout bubbled from his slack mouth and spread in a frothy pool across the beige carpet.

Getting to his feet, Encizo kicked the fallen Uzi across the room, then walked to the door. He met James in the doorway. The ex-SWAT man handed Encizo his MP-5 and glanced at the ruin of a dead man without a word.

Together they walked along the passage until they reached room 12. There was a key in the door. James turned it and pushed open the door.

Peering into the room, the Phoenix pair saw an attractive dark-haired woman who looked to be in her late thirties, sitting on the edge of the bed. Standing next to her was a slim, pretty girl of around sixteen. The girl was a younger version of her mother, with the same dark hair and striking features.

"Mrs. Harriman?" Encizo asked gently.

"Yes," the woman said. Her voice was a little shaky, but there was still a lot of fight left in her tone.

Calvin James smiled. "Sorry about the noise, ma'am. But that's all over now. We've come to take you home."

"Is my husband safe? Has he been rescued?" Julie Harriman asked with hope in her voice.

"Not yet. We have people handling that right now," Encizo said.

"One of them made contact with your husband a short time back," James said. "He was hanging on."

"He will be all right, won't he?" the girl asked in a pleading, tremulous voice. She was obviously quite shaken up.

"Everyone involved is doing their best," Encizo said to reassure her a little bit.

"Mrs. Harriman, we were told there was a caretaker in the building," James said inquiringly, and she nodded in answer.

"There was. Soon after they brought us here, they showed us his body. It wasn't very nice what they had done to him. The reason they did it was to show us they meant business, they said."

"I wish we could have spared you that," Encizo said.

"Don't apologize. At least we have made it," she said as she stood up, and mother and daughter gave each other a brief hug, knowing they were lucky to have emerged alive from their ordeal.

Encizo nodded. He glanced at James. "Go and signal the chopper. Then let's get out of here."

20

"Has he talked?" Dexter asked as he entered the room. He was referring to the RBP captive they had brought back to the safehouse and who was now secure in a basement room.

McCarter glanced up from pouring himself a mug of black coffee. "Some," he said.

"Anything useful?"

"He doesn't know where this up-country base is. Just that it's well north of London."

"Well, maybe we can tie that in with the information I've collected," Dexter said, indicating a thin folder he was carrying.

Katz gathered the rest of the force to the table where Dexter was laying out his information sheets.

"It struck me that the base the RBP used in Rainham wasn't just somewhere they happened to find. You don't just walk in and set up. You need electricity connected, and the telephone.

"So I did some checking. The industrial site is owned by a huge business group belonging to the Max Henderson empire. Multimillionaire with a hand in all kinds of things. Now Henderson is a devout capitalist. He just loves making money and spends most of his time abroad chasing more. He's known in the City and belongs to the best clubs."

"Doesn't sound the sort who would mix with the RBP," Karl Hahn said.

"No chance," Dexter affirmed. "The RBP stands for everything Henderson despises."

"But?" Katz said.

Dexter tapped one of his information sheets. "Max Henderson has a twenty-five-year-old son called Steven. He works in the company headquarters in London and has a responsible position and a fair amount of clout. What Max Henderson doesn't know, but Special Branch found out, is that our boy Steven is secretly a member of the RBP. If his old man found out, he'd have the kid's ass kicked all the way to the gutter."

"How deep in is Henderson, Junior?" McCarter asked.

"He's a card-carrying member. As I said, though, he stays in the background. Never gets involved in any of the marches or demonstrations." Dexter scanned a typed report. "Special Branch figures he provides financial and material support. That kind of thing."

"Do we have anything that will connect him with the Rainham base?" Katz asked.

"We do now," Dexter said triumphantly. "We put our computers to work. They traced an account with the electricity company for the Rainham base back to Steven Henderson, via one of Henderson International's subsidiary companies. Our next move was to repeat the exercise, this time with British Telecom. Same result. A telephone account opened via Steven Henderson."

"I'll bet the bugger hasn't paid his bloody bill," McCarter muttered in the background.

A smiling Dexter produced a computer readout tear sheet. "One thing they couldn't avoid," he said. "The telephone company's record of all calls made from the Rainham base."

"They must have figured themselves pretty secure to go making phone calls," Gary Manning said.

"Why not?" Katz replied. "The Rainham base wasn't registered to the RBP. It was pretty isolated and they weren't planning on staying all that long. It was a calculated risk they had to take in order to keep in contact with all their outside people."

"There were a number of calls to the RBP headquarters in Islington," Dexter explained. "A couple to the United States. The number turned out to be an empty apartment in New York."

"I'll bet we could link that to our Mafia connection," Katz said.

"The most interesting calls were to a number we traced to a large country estate in Derbyshire," Dexter said.

"Which, incidentally, is way north of London," McCarter said, brightening a little with the hint of possible action.

"The estate is in the Peak District National Park area of the county," Dexter explained. "Look." He unfolded a large map. "It's pretty wild terrain up there. Bleak in the winter. Hills and plenty of woodland. Stretches of moorland." He jabbed a finger at the map. "The actual estate used to belong to the Laxdale family. Titled bunch that go way back. The title lapsed a few years ago because there were no heirs. The sole surviving Laxdale decided to sell, and guess who bought the place?"

"Henderson International?" Hahn volunteered.

"Right. They were going to develop it as a tourist park, but Max Henderson can't make up his mind how to approach the project. At present the estate is standing empty. Big house and outbuildings. Farmland. Forest. Hundreds of acres in a remote corner of the county. The nearest village is almost twenty miles away."

"An ideal place for hiding four mobile missile units while you prepare them for firing," Manning said.

At that moment the telephone rang, and Katz answered it. "Green speaking," he acknowledged.

"I've good news," Hal Brognola said, his voice as clear as if he were standing in the room next to Katz.

"We could do with some," the Phoenix commander said.

"I heard from Calvin and Rafael a short while ago," the Fed said. "They have Harriman's wife and daughter safe and well."

"Good work," Katz exclaimed. "Though it won't help the man himself at the moment."

"I have something that might help *you*," Brognola said. "One of the kidnappers, now deceased, had on him what we've now confirmed as a telephone number. It was written on a slip of paper he had in his wallet. Probably did it because the combination was for a foreign exchange."

"Is it for a location in England?" Katz asked.

"Yeah," Brognola said.

"Hold on a moment," Katz said. He glanced at Hahn. "Blue, bring a sheet of paper and a pen." While he waited for Hahn to join him, Katz turned to the others. "Mrs. Harriman and her daughter are in safe hands."

"Great!" Manning said.

Hahn passed the writing materials to Katz, who proceeded to give Brognola the go-ahead. "All right, give me the number."

"That it?" Katz asked after he'd finished jotting it down.

"Yes. Does it help?"

"Hold on while we see if it's useful to Dexter," Katz instructed.

It took only a few seconds for Dexter to check the number against his own list. "It's the number for the Laxdale estate," he announced.

"Thanks," Katz said to Brognola. "It confirms our location of the main base from where we suspect the RBP terrorists intend launching the Manta missiles."

"Well, you know what to do," Brognola growled. "Take 'em out."

"We'll handle it," Katz assured him.

"I know you will. Yakov, good luck."

"I'll be in touch."

Katz replaced the telephone, found his package of cigarettes and after fishing one out, lit it. "Let's gear up," he said. "Dexter, how long will it take us to drive to this Laxdale estate?"

"You'll do it in just over three hours," Dexter said. "The major part of the journey can be done on the M1 motorway."

He bent over the map again, tracing the route for Katz. "Mr. White, as you are familiar with the road system, you'd better be in on this," Dexter suggested.

McCarter joined them. "Am I the chauffeur this trip?"

"Yes," Katz told him.

"But please spare us your usual manner of driving," Gary Manning reminded his teammate. "We want to get there in one piece."

"Just hold your breath," McCarter said with a wicked grin, concentrating on the map and the route that would take Phoenix Force to the confrontation with the RBP. A confrontation from which they would have to emerge as winners.

21

"I demand to know what's going on!" Vernon Harrap ranted.

Lubichek quietly closed the door behind the RBP leader as Harrap pushed his way into the room and strode up to Alex Manson.

"Well?" Harrap shrilled. When he became angry his nasal voice rose to an almost feminine whine.

Manson, who was standing at one of the recessed windows of the room that had once been the library of the Laxdale mansion, turned slowly. His eyes were hard and angry, showing none of the tolerance he had formerly displayed in front of the fanatical RBP headman. "Surely you know what's happening," Manson said. "After all, you are in charge around here."

Harrap was caught off guard. He fell silent, eyeing Manson with deepening suspicion. "Who are those foreigners working on the missiles?"

"Just technicians," Lubichek said.

"Doing what?"

"You wouldn't understand," Lubichek told him.

"I wasn't told about them," Harrap said. "And why all the secrecy? No one is allowed near the missiles." He banged his fist on the windowsill. "I want to know what's going on! Too much is happening I don't know anything about. People being killed all over the place. This house and the grounds—it's like an armed camp.''

"Because that is precisely what it is," Manson snapped.

"I'm beginning to wonder just what you two have to hide," Harrap said. "I don't believe you've told me everything."

"And I was certain we had," Lubichek said. "You haven't kept anything from our dear comrade, have you?" he asked, turning to Manson with a smile.

"Come to think of it, perhaps there are a few points I didn't cover," the renegade admitted.

"Such as?" Harrap asked.

"Such as the fact that as of now you've just stepped down as head of the RBP," Manson said.

"Don't be so absurd." Harrap laughed. "I *am* the RBP!"

"No, Vernon," Lubichek said. "You are simply an embarrassing joke."

Harrap glanced at the two men. What he saw caused suspicion, then realization to dawn on his face. "You bastards!" he yelled. "I've been used. All those promises, those fancy words. You didn't mean a single thing you said."

"I promised you that the RBP would be remembered," Lubichek reminded him. "And it will."

"For what?" Harrap demanded to know. "You said the missiles would be used to express the party's commitment. They would be exploded to create panic and confusion. To give us the opportunity to strike at the government. What is your real intention for the missiles? Damn it, I demand you tell me!"

"Very well, Vernon," Lubichek said. He walked around to stand on Harrap's left, giving Manson a slight nod when he was briefly out of Harrap's line of vision.

"The foreigners, as you call them, are technicians from Libya. At this moment they are arming the Manta missiles with low-yield nuclear warheads. When we finally persuade Harriman to access the missile computers, we will be able to program the missiles onto the targets we have selected."

"United States Air Force bases here in Britain," Manson explained. "Four of the biggest have been chosen. They will be erased completely, as will all personnel and armaments."

Harrap stared at them, his eyes mirroring the horror he felt. "My God, you're both mad! Completely mad!"

"But it's what you wanted," Lubichek taunted. "A direct blow against the government and the American warmongers they collaborate with."

"Nuclear strikes? It's lunacy!" Harrap yelled. "You'll turn the country into a radioactive wasteland. Thousands could die. Overturn the government, yes, but not by destroying the country. What use would it be to anyone? Don't you fools know something like this could escalate? It could bring about retaliation."

"What a naive fool you are," Lubichek sneered. "Do you really think I care about your moronic little group? Or a few thousand dead! None of it matters on the scale of the real struggle. With these missiles we can wipe out NATO credibility. Destroy some of their strongest bases. Cause dissent among the allies. And all you care about is your stupid little party."

Harrap turned on Manson. "You used my people. Let them do your dirty work, got them slaughtered."

"No more than they deserved," Manson said. "A bunch of has-beens. Street thugs with shit for brains." He laughed. "All I had to do was toss them a few shiny guns, and they all thought they were Rambo."

The stark truth assumed nightmarish proportions before Vernon Harrap's eyes. He saw fully how he had been taken for a ride. Manson and Lubichek had convinced him of their sincerity, while all the time they were just playing on his fanatic zeal, and he had been swept along on a rosy cloud. The only reason for it all had been their need for a ready-formed group to provide men and contacts. Harrap had been convinced, and in turn he had told his people to follow. Which they were still doing.

It had to stop! Now! Harrap thought frantically and turned and ran for the door. The door was almost within reach when he felt a powerful hand grip his right shoulder. He was spun around.

Alex Manson was standing before him, a cold gleam in his eyes. "Nowhere left to go, sucker," he said.

"No!" Harrap screamed.

The knife in Manson's hand flashed in the afternoon light. The keen edge of the blade slashed across Harrap's neck, laying it open from ear to ear. The wound was deep, slicing through flesh and muscle and severing the trachea. Blood welled up instantly, spilling from the gaping wound in a torrent. Harrap's instinctive reaction was to clamp his hands to his neck, in the belief it might stop the streams of blood. It was a wasted effort. He sagged back against the wall and slid to the floor. The front of his white shirt was drenched, as were his hands. His body shuddered and arched for a time, while wet gurgling sounds bubbled from his gaping throat. His movement became weaker as his pounding heart continued to pump blood from the great wound in his throat.

Manson had already turned away from the dying man. After wiping it, he put the knife away and cast a glance at the waiting Lubichek.

"I wish our problems with Phillip Harriman could be resolved as easily," Lubichek remarked.

"Maybe another lesson in persuasion will help," Manson said as they left the room. He locked the door and put the key into his pocket.

They proceeded to make their way through the empty, echoing mansion along corridors hung with old oil paintings. But neither man gave the pictures a passing glance. Their minds were on other things.

As they passed a small room with its doors wide open, Manson's man Landis called to them.

"Any change?" Manson asked him.

Landis shook his head. "I've repeatedly tried both numbers. No answer from either the RBP headquarters in London, or the people in New Mexico."

"Shit!" Manson exclaimed in frustration. "I'm starting to feel somebody walking in my shadow."

"Let us concentrate on Harriman," Lubichek said. "If we can break him we may still achieve our aim, Alex."

"And if we don't?"

"We must be optimistic," the Russian said. "The game is not over until the last shot has been fired."

"Depends who gets hit by it," Manson observed.

They continued through the mansion and reached a lower level of the rambling building. A short flight of stone steps led to a door giving access to a low-ceilinged stone-floored room that had been equipped at some earlier time as a workshop. An armed guard stood outside the door.

It was the room where Phillip Harriman lay strapped naked to a heavy wooden workbench.

"So, Phillip, we can now devote ourselves to you," Lubichek said cheerfully. "What do you think of the decor?"

Harriman didn't respond. He fixed his gaze on a distant corner of the ceiling and tried desperately to shut everything else from his mind. The problem was it didn't work as well as it should have.

"Ah, the silent treatment," Lubichek said. "I think we have a cure for that." He moved to the large board fixed to the wall and made a show of rummaging among the varied selection of tools clipped to the board.

"I am sure, Phillip, that you are aware of the diversity of the sensation we call pain. It can range from a mere pinprick up to the most terrible agony. In between are many degrees of intensity and duration. Man has many levels of resistance to pain. The average man does not know his own pain threshold until he is put to the test. Some people can resist great pain while others are broken by very little. You, Phillip, have stood up quite well. However, we now have the time and the opportunity to find your limits."

Lubichek returned to the bench and positioned himself so that he was in Harriman's view and also afforded the American a look at what he held in his hand.

The Russian had a pair of large pliers in his hand. He opened the metal jaws, then closed them with a sudden snap.

"I think we will start with these."

He leaned over Harriman's naked body, tracing a line across the taut stomach with the cold metal of the pliers. The feel of the pliers made Harriman shudder. He felt them glide lightly down into his groin. Then the contact vanished.

But only for a moment, just until Lubichek closed the cruel jaws over vulnerable, sensitive flesh and gripped hard. Twisted. Pulled.

Sudden excruciating pain flared through Harriman's nervous system. He arched up off the bench, straining against the leather straps holding him helpless. As the pain went on and on, he tried to control himself but was finally unable to hold back a shriek of agony. The sound dissolved into a quivering sob that broke from his trembling lips.

And then the pain ceased.

Harriman flopped back on the bench. Sweat poured from his body. He was trembling uncontrollably. There was a pulsing, burning pain in his groin where Lubichek's pliers had done their work.

The KGB man's face loomed over the bench, suspended above Harriman. The Russian was smiling. "It amazes me what a man will endure in the name of loyalty."

"You're a bastard," Harriman moaned.

"Not true," Lubichek said. "My parents were very married." He chuckled at his own humor.

"You want me to call New Mexico?" Manson asked, keeping up the pretense of still being in contact with the kidnappers. "We could let them loose on the kid. The guys would have a hell of a time working on her with a pair of pliers."

"An excellent suggestion," Lubichek agreed. "Perhaps we could even allow Phillip to listen in on an extension."

Harriman fought against his restraints, oblivious to the pain his struggles were causing. The leather straps cut into his wrists and ankles, chafing and tearing the flesh until it bled. "Let me loose, you sons of bitches!" he screamed. "I'll kill you with my bare hands!"

"You can end all this suffering for your family and yourself," Lubichek said softly. "Simply cooperate and everything will be all right. It's so simple, Phillip. All you have to do is access the Manta computers and let us take over."

"And then what? You'll let me go free? Do I look stupid?"

"You talk stupid," Manson snapped. "Listen and listen good, Harriman. Do what Lubichek wants, or I will let those goons in New Mexico have a go at your wife and kid. I promise you they'll make it last. Those boys are real animals. They'll have a hell of a time with that sixteen-year-old kid of yours. They may be dumb, but when it comes to women, they've got some imagination."

Harriman's mind whirled. He was sick with pain and fear. He could hardly bear to think of his wife and daughter and the pain and humiliation they might have to suffer. And all because of the damned missiles.

Lubichek's timing served to heighten the mental torture along with the physical. The brief respite intensified the anticipation of pain, making it greater and harder to bear. The KGB man bent to his task again, the pliers doing their insidious work. The screams that erupted from Phillip Harriman's throat were wrenched from the bottom of his very soul.

The sight and sound of the torture had no effect on Alex Manson. He had seen it all before, and had been involved, during his Vietnam tours.

What did trouble Manson was the communication breakdown between bases. Something was happening. In Manson's mind lurked the specter of enemy involvement. In this instance *enemy* meant security forces. He had not forgotten the man named McCarter. His escape had been a breach of RBP security that might have led to further attacks on the London headquarters and the New Mexico base. It was foolish to imagine that the authorities were not doing anything to try and recover both the hijacked missiles and the kidnapped Harrimans. It was entirely possible that McCarter was part of some security operation already under way.

The Laxdale estate could come under attack if the security force managed to obtain its location. Manson knew from past experience that there was no such thing as one-hundred-percent secrecy.

He was also encumbered with the RBP fanatics, who were something less than professional. However, that was something he had to live with. He had accepted the RBP's involvement at the start, and there was no way of dispensing with them now. If trouble did start, he would need them, regardless of their inadequacy.

It would be a case of holding out for as long as possible. There was still a chance Lubichek might coax Harriman into cooperating. Manson had to admit the likelihood of that was getting slimmer all the time, but it was still worth hanging on to until the last moment.

If the inevitable happened and the project had to be abandoned, there was a standby helicopter waiting behind the house.

The thought of the project's breaking down stayed in Manson's mind and refused to go away. Manson was a practical man, and as such he knew that sometimes failure had to be accepted. It could come about despite preplanning and initial on-target execution of a project. He knew he would have a bitter pill to swallow if the project was destroyed. The outcome of launching the Manta missiles would have been interesting to observe, and the consequences still were hard to imagine because there were so many variables to the scenarios that could follow.

Manson's train of thought halted as he became aware of silence instead of Harriman's screaming. He glanced across at Lubichek.

The Russian was shaking his bald head slowly. Sweat glistened on his taut face. "He has passed out," he said, a trace of annoyance in his voice. "Now I will have to wait until he recovers. Such a nuisance."

"I'm going to take a look around the grounds," Manson said.

Lubichek nodded absently. He was engrossed in choosing another tool from the wall rack.

Leaving the room, Manson made his way back upstairs to the large entrance hall. He picked up his Ingram MAC-10 from a small table and checked to see that it was ready for use.

He was just reaching for the ornate handle on the heavy front door when he heard the distant but unmistakable crackle of full-auto fire. A moment later more gunfire erupted from another section of the grounds.

For an instant Alex Manson froze. His worst fears appeared to have come true. The base was under attack. From the proximity of the gunfire it seemed that the grounds had been breached. Unless some miracle took place and this attack force was eliminated, then the Manta project was doomed. If that happened, Manson's own dream of power and glory would die, too. But he could live with that. It was not beyond reason to expect another opportunity to arise. So the need was to survive. To live for another day. A wasted life was over for good once the fatal bullet hit home. To cut and run if the odds became too short was sound strategy.

But the moment passed and Manson's military side took over, rising to the challenge. The sound of battle. He felt the old heat surge in his blood. Felt the pounding drive return and knew that the day was not yet lost.

Whoever it was who made up the unknown attack force had a battle ahead, because Alex Manson had a lot of fight left in him.

He slammed open the door, yelling over his shoulder for Landis to move his ass, then stepped outside, squinting his eyes against the afternoon sun as he sought the enemy.

22

The Range Rover had been parked by McCarter out of sight in a deep copse where the canopy of treetops created a near solid covering. Little sunlight reached the ground, where fern and grass grew in rich abundance. The shadowed coolness seemed to merge with the silence that lay over the place.

The Laxdale estate was a quarter of a mile away. A high stone wall formed the estate's boundary where it ran parallel with the narrow country road. Flanked by wide carved stone pillars, a pair of massive wrought-iron gates shut off the entrance to the drive leading into the estate.

After McCarter had parked the Rover and cut the engine, Katz had called a final briefing. "We want to bring Phillip Harriman out alive if possible," he said. "There is, however, a much more urgent consideration. The RBP terrorists are planning to launch the Manta missiles, on unspecified and unsuspecting targets, fitted with nuclear warheads. The implications are clear—a total disregard for human life, which, unfortunately, is part of the terrorist psyche. The terrorist doesn't consider the effects, mental or physical, of his antisocial act. If he does think about it, he doesn't care what happens to the innocent victims. With that in mind, we have to stop the RBP's insane plan. That is our priority. As for the terrorists, they have, by their actions, forfeited any right to humane considerations."

"In other words, if they get in the way," McCarter said, "we take them out."

Katz nodded. "As the old expression goes—no quarter."

Gary Manning and Karl Hahn moved out to take a look at the perimeter defenses. They were back in just over twenty minutes. "No electronics as far as we could see," Hahn reported. "I don't think they've had time to install anything sophisticated."

"We spotted two armed guards on the gate," Manning said. "And there appear to be a couple more roving around the grounds near the wall."

"All right," Katz said. "They have to be dealt with first."

Manning removed his Anschutz air rifle from its case. The Anschutz was a high-quality precision rifle, and in Manning's capable hands it became a deadly accurate weapon. Loaded with hypodarts that injected Thorazine, the Anschutz could put a target to sleep in seconds.

"This should get us our entrance tickets," the Canadian said.

"Just make sure you don't shoot yourself in the foot," McCarter commented dryly.

The Briton was smoking one of his favorite Player's cigarettes, seemingly unaffected by the three-hour, high-speed drive he had just made from London. It said a lot for his stamina that despite all he'd been through, plus the irritation of his shoulder wound, McCarter was his usual cheerfully gruff, irreverent self.

One by one Phoenix Force left the Range Rover, taking time to give their weapons a final check. They were all packing extra ammunition in their belt pouches. In addition to their handguns and SMGs the commando warriors had clipped M-26 grenades to their belts. They were going in after the RBP with all guns blazing, knowing full well that there would be no second chance. The threat of the Manta missiles armed with nuke warheads was the spur that would initiate Phoenix Force's attack on the terrorist base.

They set off through the thick undergrowth, their camouflage combat dress blending in with the greenery. Manning led, followed by Katz and Hahn. McCarter brought up the rear.

The quarter mile to the Laxdale estate was covered quickly, and Phoenix Force was soon studying the walled enclosure. Across the road from their place of concealment was the entrance to the estate, with the two SMG-armed guards visible behind the wrought-iron gates.

Gary Manning found himself a comfortable spot and raised the loaded Anschutz. The rifle was fitted with a Bushnell scope, a sight the Canadian had used many times before. He selected his first target, patiently waiting for the right moment. It came when the target's partner bent his head to light a cigarette. At that moment Manning pulled the trigger, and the Anschutz expelled its dart. The tiny missile struck its target in the side of the neck. The guard stiffened and put his hand up to the stinging spot. Then he slumped forward against the iron gates and began to slide to the ground.

The second guard finally looked up from lighting his smoke. He saw his buddy already falling to the ground. Unsure of what was happening, he stood and stared, while his mind got itself in gear. A second later he, too, felt a sharp stabbing sensation in his neck. As the Thorazine did its speedy work, the guard joined his partner on the ground.

For the moment the gate was clear, but there was no telling how long it would remain so. The Phoenix warriors broke out of the undergrowth and sprinted across the road.

Karl Hahn, with a boost from Manning, scaled the wall. He flattened himself on the wide top, checking that the coast was clear, then dropped out of sight on the far side. Moments later he appeared at the gates where he slid free the heavy bolt securing the gates, pulling them open to allow the rest of the team inside.

The unconscious guards were stripped of all their weapons, then cuffed and gagged. The secured men were dragged out of sight behind the thick bushes that fringed the drive.

"We'll head for the house," Katz said. "According to those plans Dexter showed us, the outbuildings are on the far side of the house. There are a couple of large storage sheds where the Manta units could be concealed."

There was plenty of cover as Phoenix Force moved forward. Stands of trees and abundant undergrowth spread across the grounds.

It was McCarter who spotted the first of the roving guards. The SAS veteran caught a glimpse of the RBP terrorist as he stepped into a wide clearing. The guard was carrying an AK-47, slung over his shoulder by its webbing strap.

McCarter signaled for the other force members to stay put. He edged forward, moving silently from cover to cover, angling in toward the unsuspecting terrorist.

From his cover, McCarter took stock of the the RBP man. He seemed to be feeling pretty good about things, and there was a contented look on his face. The AK-47 he carried made him feel taller and stronger, just the way he had felt when he had had a go at Harriman. With admiration he unslung the weapon from his shoulder and inspected it fondly, hoping he would get an opportunity to use it.

But that opportunity was suddenly and rudely wrested from him. The Russian-made weapon was destined to stay silent.

McCarter lunged out of the undergrowth and confronted the surprised terrorist. The Brit's right fist struck a single devastating blow directly over Judson's temple, breaking the sphenoid bone. Such was the force of the blow that it pushed a jagged shard of bone deep into Judson's brain. The massive shock from the injury pushed the terrorist toward a swift death, his body shuddering in spasms as he collapsed on the ground. He died without uttering a sound or even being aware of what had happened.

As the terrorist dropped, McCarter waved to his partners and pushed forward, increasing his pace.

"Here we go again," grumbled Manning. He slung his Anschutz across his back by its sling and hefted the 9 mm Uzi he had chosen for his main assault weapon.

They continued through the trees and undergrowth for another few hundred yards. After that the ground became more open.

It was then that a second roving guard stepped from cover and came face-to-face with Phoenix Force. The man reacted with surprising speed, whipping up his Uzi SMG and opening fire. His first and only burst kicked up a ragged line of holes in the ground.

Katz, displaying his usual speed and dexterity, returned fire. His volley stitched a series of bloody holes in the guard's torso and sent the surprised man down in a welter of blood to writhe briefly in the grass before death claimed him.

McCarter glanced from the corpse to Katz. "I think that little exchange may have given us away," he said.

"No point in being quiet any longer," Katz responded.

They broke from the undergrowth and sprinted across the untended lawns—and ran head-on into the opposition.

Armed RBP terrorists burst from various points around the house, firing as they came. The reckless RBP men expended a great deal of ammunition to little effect. Evidently the trigger-happy fanatics had failed to learn it takes a good shot to hit a target while on the move, and even more so when wielding a fast-firing SMG.

Phoenix Force split apart, spreading across the wide lawns.

Karl Hahn opened fire with his MP-5, raking a pair of yelling men, who tumbled to the ground in a mini-explosion of tattered flesh and shattered bone. The self-styled storm troopers died as they had lived—creating a lot of noise and leaving an untidy mess where they fell.

A heavyset terrorist with a stubby mat-black MAC-10 took aim at Gary Manning's weaving figure. The burst of fire sailed over the Canadian's head. Manning instantly dropped to one knee, raising his Uzi. He had the weapon set on single shot, and one was all he needed. The projectile whizzed through the air and crashed into his opponent's head directly between the eyes. Coring through the brain, it burst its way out of the back of the skull. The dead terrorist sprawled facedown in the grass.

To the left of Manning, finding himself closer to the house, Katz saw a tight group of RBP men approaching from the far side of the half-dozen cars parked on the wide graveled drive. Letting his Uzi dangle by its strap, the Israeli pulled an M-26 fragmentation grenade from his belt. He pulled the pin with the tip of his prosthesis hook, then expertly lobbed the grenade under one of the cars as the terrorists passed it.

The explosion caught the enemy unaware. They were hurled in all directions by the blast, bodies ripped and pulped by the flying debris from the grenade and the car as the gasoline tank blew. Blazing fuel sprayed the yelling, bleeding terrorists, turning two of them into human torches. They ran screaming from the explosion, only increasing their agony as they fanned the flames eating at their flesh. Katz ended their misery with a sharp burst of autofire.

Rounding the blazing wreck of the car, Katz unleashed a further rain of death from his Uzi, finishing what the grenade had started. RBP terrorists were blown to bloody rags by the Israeli's accurate fire. His final burst ended the budding career of the last man in the group and his life along with it, spilling his blood into the dirt.

David McCarter had tossed a grenade himself, igniting a couple more of the parked cars. The explosions and the flaming of spilled gasoline added to the confusion and noise. Fire and smoke belched from the wrecked vehicles, issuing across the area as a slight breeze caught it.

McCarter shot the legs out from under a terrorist who loomed out of the smoke, then ducked to avoid a butt stroke aimed at him. Before the terrorist could turn on him again, McCarter kicked him hard between his legs. The man doubled over, and the full force of McCarter's knee connected with the fanatic's face with a crunching of bones. Clutching his ruined face, the terrorist stumbled away from McCarter. The Briton punched a short burst from the Ingram through his chest to spread him flat on the ground.

Yet another of the parked cars burst apart as an overheated fuel tank blew. A writhing ball of flame billowed skyward. Debris rained down on the RBP terrorists and Phoenix Force alike.

Making a wide circuit around the blazing cars, McCarter spotted a familiar face. Alex Manson!

The renegade was urging his RBP force to carry the battle forward but seemed to be having little success. His troops were not disciplined professionals. They were street scum more used to jumping someone in a dark alley, and though they were attempting to fight back, their lack of combat experience was in evidence.

By a quirk of fate Manson looked in McCarter's direction in the same moment. Their eyes locked, and despite the drifting smoke swirling between them, McCarter saw the bitter expression that filled the deserter's eyes.

Manson threw up his own Ingram and cut loose with an angry burst in the Phoenix warrior's direction. Bullets hummed through the air, coming close to McCarter, but not mowing him down because he had anticipated Manson's move. He hurled himself behind one of the burning cars, ignoring the heat that stung his face as Manson fired again. Hot slugs clanged against the fire-scorched body of the car concealing McCarter.

Aware that he couldn't stay where he was, McCarter scrambled toward the rear of the car. He dodged through the gap between two of the shattered hulks, almost tripping over the charred body of a terrorist who had been caught by one of the grenade blasts.

Peering around the rear of the car, McCarter saw Manson and another man in the act of dodging back inside the house.

"You don't get off that easy!" the Briton muttered as he jammed a fresh magazine into the MAC-10, then made a dash for the house.

One of the retreating men spun around, brandishing a big .357 Magnum revolver. He jerked the muzzle down at McCarter and pulled the trigger. The screaming projectile burned air near McCarter's head.

McCarter had ducked below the gun's barrel, still moving forward, and he cannoned into the fanatic, who snarled as McCarter grabbed his waist and kept on pushing. The forward motion knocked them off balance, and locked together, the pair hit one of the windows flanking the main doors. There was a crash of breaking glass as McCarter and his human shield hurtled over the windowsill and disappeared inside.

The terrorist who lunged at Gary Manning was a six-foot-six giant with massive arms and chest. He held a mini-Uzi in one large fist, and the moment he set eyes on Manning he pulled the trigger of the compact weapon. The mini-Uzi spit out its stream of death dealers in a continuous blast of sound. If the RBP fanatic had taken a fraction longer to aim, he might have scored a hit. But he had missed his opportunity, because the tough Canadian hauled his own SMG into play and squeezed the trigger the moment the muzzle was lined up. Burning slugs tore into the terrorist's side to cleave flesh and bone, ripping his torso open by the awesome power of the blast. The man fell in a stiff-boned manner, like a puppet on its last legs.

Without a pause Manning ran on while expending the Uzi's magazine at another RBP foe, who staggered away with mortal wounds.

Rounding the side of the great house, Manning saw where the ground sloped away toward a cluster of buildings some distance away. He flattened himself against the stone wall of the house and ejected the empty magazine from the Uzi. With calm deliberation he fed in a fresh one and recocked the SMG.

A shadow fell across the ground. Manning whipped up the Uzi, then saw that it was Katz. The Israeli indicated the buildings with his prosthesis.

"The missiles?" he suggested.

"Could be," Manning said. "Shall we take a look?"

They angled across the slope, approaching the buildings along their blind side.

The gunfire around the house had ceased. Only the crackle of the burning cars disturbed the sudden silence. A heavy pall of dark smoke had risen into the sky.

Manning touched Katz's shoulder to call his attention to a figure moving past a tangle of undergrowth off to their left.

"It's Karl," he said to Katz.

The Israeli whistled to catch the German's attention, then indicated the cluster of buildings. Hahn raised an arm in understanding.

"Where's David?" Manning asked, having lost sight of McCarter during the hectic race for the house.

"Dealing with some business inside the house," said Katz, who had witnessed McCarter's unusual method of entry into the Laxdale mansion.

"Off enjoying himself again," Manning commented dryly.

"Whatever it is he'll handle it," Katz said. "Now let's find those blasted missiles!"

ALTHOUGH THE TERRORIST beneath McCarter had taken the brunt of the fall through the window and the subsequent hard landing on the floor of the room beyond, he had retained enough strength to fight back.

As the terrorist hit the floor, the Magnum spun from his fingers. Frantically he arched his solid body up from the floor, throwing McCarter clear, then twisted himself toward the Magnum.

McCarter rolled to his feet the moment he collided with the floor, realizing that the terrorist was going for his gun. Gathering his reserves, the Phoenix pro launched himself through the air.

The terrorist's hand had barely closed over the Magnum's butt when McCarter's combat boot smashed down on it, crushing flesh and bone alike. Blood squirted from split fingers, and turning his face up toward McCarter, the terrorist loosed off a stream of foul language. All that got him was the hard crunch of McCarter's boot alongside his jaw. The man's head whipped to the side, and the terrific force of the kick snapped his neck like a dry twig.

McCarter glanced around the room, searching for the door. The first thing he saw was the bloody corpse of Vernon Harrap. The dead RBP leader's throat had been laid open from ear to ear. Judging by the state of the blood that had spilled from the huge wound, Harrap had not been dead very long.

Who, the Cockney rebel wondered, had cut Harrap's lifeline? The guy's death had nothing to do with Phoenix Force and it was unlikely that the RBP's prisoner, Phillip Harriman, would have carried out such a cold-blooded slaughter. Had Manson and the KGB man been conniving to rid themselves of the RBP headman once they reached a certain point in their project? McCarter was aware there were a lot of questions he could have asked. Too many, and none of them were really going to help him.

McCarter figured that Harrap's death was the result of an internal dispute. Maybe a falling-out between members of the hierarchy. He recalled the way Lubichek and Manson had treated Harrap back at the Islington base.

It was time to press on. McCarter tried the door and found it was locked. The Phoenix fighting machine didn't hesitate. He used his Ingram to blast the lock apart, then booted the door open. As it swung open, he plunged through into the depths of Laxdale mansion.

McCarter's objectives were all linked together. He wanted to find Phillip Harriman and keep the promise he had made to the man. He also wanted Alex Manson. The renegade was obviously the driving force behind the RBP's acts of violence—one of which had been the murder of Jake Tasker, as well as the slaughter of the soldiers guarding the Manta units.

Manson had built up a catalog of bad debts, and McCarter decided it was time to have them settled in full.

He reached the once-polished oak floor of the spacious entrance hall. A wide curving staircase led to the upper floors.

The faint sound of receding footsteps reached McCarter's ears. He whirled around noiselessly and spotted an armed figure slipping through a paneled door at the far end of the hall.

McCarter followed until he reached the partly open door where he paused, his MAC-10 up and ready. From the other side of the door he could still hear distant footsteps.

The impulsive Briton put his foot to the door and kicked it wide open, sending it crashing back against the wall. Almost at once an SMG opened fire, and slugs whacked the oak doorframe inches from McCarter's face. He hastily pulled his head back as splinters of wood exploded around him.

He had seen what lay beyond the door in the instant before the burst of gunfire—a long hallway, its walls covered in veneered wood panels.

The combat veteran knew he had no time to waste. He snatched a grenade from his belt and yanked the pin. He popped the lever, held the M-26 for a second, then rolled it along the passage floor.

When it came the explosion seemed to rock the entire house. The detonating grenade lit up the hall for an instant, followed by the crash of the explosion. Dust and smoke billowed along the corridor, and McCarter used it as his cover. He dashed into the hallway, his shoulders hunched against the falling debris, his long legs carrying him swiftly along. Through the pale wreaths of smoke he made out a staggering figure.

McCarter kept moving, his Ingram tracking the unsteady form. Then he cleared the pall of smoke and saw his quarry some yards ahead. Apparently caught by fragments from the M-26, the man was clutching a shoulder that was a pulpy, bleeding mess.

The injured man was Landis, a member of Manson's renegade team. The grenade had caught him unprepared, and he'd had no time to completely evade it. His only hope of protection had been to flatten himself against the corridor wall. Actually he'd been lucky. His right shoulder had stopped some of the grenade blast, and the rest of him had been untouched.

Turning on his heel as he heard his pursuer coming on, Landis caught a glimpse of the fox-faced Briton pounding along the passage like some raging juggernaut.

Landis understood he had one chance left, and a slim one at that. He made to lift his 9 mm Uzi, forgetting his wounded shoulder. Punishing pain flared when he began to lift the SMG, and the shrapnel-damaged muscle refused to respond as it would have normally. He pulled the Uzi's trigger a fraction too soon, blasting a ragged line of holes in the oak floor.

McCarter, his Ingram still tracked in on the terrorist, returned fire. The sustained blast raked Landis from hip to collarbone. Landis was slapped off balance, and he bounced against the paneled wall before losing control of his limbs and crashing to the floor in a twitching heap.

McCarter ejected the Ingram's magazine and snapped in a fresh one. He cocked the weapon and looked beyond the dead man to check out what lay ahead.

The end of the passage formed a T-junction. The right arm of the T ended in an open door and a flight of steps leading down to a lower level of the house. The steps themselves were stone, the edges worn from many years of use.

McCarter caught the murmur of voices and plunged down the steps two at a time. He was halfway down the flight when an armed terrorist burst into view. Seeing the Phoenix pro, the man opened fire immediately with the H&K MP-5 he was carrying.

A stream of slugs ricocheted from the stone wall near McCarter's head, spitting needle-sharp chips into the side of his face. He responded instinctively, releasing a long burst from his Ingram. The slugs ripped into the hard-liner's head, caving in his features and scrambling the contents of his skull. Fatally hit, he tumbled back down the steps, leaving a glistening trail of blood behind him.

At the bottom of the stairs McCarter saw an open door, and from just beyond it came a rustling sound. Transferring the Ingram to his left hand, McCarter unlimbered his Browning Hi-Power. He flattened himself against the wall to one side of the door, craning his neck to peer into the room.

His view afforded him only a partial glimpse, but what he did see made his blood run cold.

Phillip Harriman lay naked on a heavy wooden bench, strapped down so his movements were restricted. Crusted as well as fresh streaks of blood and heavy bruising discolored his flesh, and his wrists were chafed raw from his vain attempts to break free from the leather restraints. McCarter saw with relief that the computer expert was still alive: Harriman's chest rose and fell with his labored breathing.

McCarter felt certain that Harriman was not alone in the room. Someone who at that moment was out of sight had been torturing the man. Which meant that Harriman still hadn't cracked. If he had agreed to access the Manta control computers, the terrorists would have had him working on the missiles. The man had told McCarter he would hang on, and the Briton's admiration for Harriman grew even more.

Silently the Phoenix pro leaned his Ingram against the wall, leaving him with the Hi-Power. One way or another he had to get into the room and take out whoever was waiting inside. There was no time for lengthy debate. The situation called for direct action, which happened to be McCarter's specialty.

He judged that the slight noise that had attracted his attention came from the right of the door. He was confident in his judgment, but well aware of the consequences of being wrong. Being who he was, McCarter decided not to second-guess himself and stuck with his decision and acted on it.

Backing away from the door, he braced himself, then made a concentrated dash for the opening. He went through the door in a low dive that took him into the room almost at floor level. As his free hand scraped the floor, McCarter curved his body around and slammed against the base of the sturdy bench on which Phillip Harriman lay.

Out of the corner of his eye the Briton had caught a flicker of movement off to his right. A moment later the heavy crash of a handgun firing filled the room with its noise. The bullet scored the stone floor inches from McCarter's prone body. A second shot came, chunking into the thick wood of the bench.

McCarter triggered two fast shots in his attacker's direction. His first clanged off some metal object. His second, which must have been closer, brought a low curse in Russian.

Lubichek, the KGB manipulator. The thought flashed into McCarter's mind as he rolled to the far end of the bench, scrambling to the opposite side. Then he rose to a crouch, his Hi-Power's muzzle seeking a target.

A swift look around revealed that he was in some kind of workshop—a tool rack on the wall, a power drill on a stand and a long work surface running the length of one wall.

There was not much to be gained from seeking cover, and without warning, McCarter rose to his full height, his eyes searching the confines of the workshop. And he pinpointed Boris Lubichek.

The Russian terror monger was at the far end of the room, pressed against the shadowed wall beside a tall metal cupboard. His bald head gleamed with perspiration, and his cold eyes glittered with rage. The Russian was bitter because his cold-blooded scheme had been interfered with. And with the instincts of a trapped animal he was seething with fury, refusing to accept defeat and more than ready to fight on.

The moment he laid eyes on the grim-faced Phoenix warrior, Lubichek swung his Makarov in McCarter's direction. The Browning fired first and kept on firing. Lubichek's stocky body was driven back against the wall as a stream of 9 mms hammered into it, opening pulpy wounds that spouted blood onto the stone floor.

McCarter stepped forward as Lubichek fell. He stood over the dying Russian as he rolled onto his side, staring up at the Phoenix warrior. The effort proved too much, and his head lolled back, his eyes rolling in their sockets.

McCarter turned to the bench where Harriman lay. He released the leather straps holding the man down and found he couldn't avoid seeing the damage Lubichek had inflicted.

There was a moment when Harriman seemed about to resist McCarter's attempt to free him, then his eyes focused and he recognized the Briton.

"Told you I'd be back," the Phoenix commando said. "Sorry it took so long."

"I didn't break," Harriman whispered. His voice was low, uneven.

"Didn't think you would," McCarter told him.

He had spotted Harriman's clothes dumped against the wall. Picking them up, McCarter placed them beside the man. "Listen, chum, I have to go. We still have to tidy things up around here. Shouldn't take long. Just bolt the door after me and don't open it until I get back."

Harriman had managed to sit up. He nodded with apparent effort. "I heard Lubichek talking to Manson about a helicopter at the back of the house, ready for a quick getaway."

"Thanks," McCarter said. "By the way, your wife and daughter are safe and well."

"Thank God," Harriman said.

Or Phoenix Force, McCarter murmured to himself irreverently as he turned to leave. "Bolt the door," he reminded Harriman as he retrieved his MAC-10. The moment he heard the bolts slide home, McCarter raced up the steps, eager to rejoin the battle.

23

As Katz and Manning closed in on the storage sheds, they were met by RBP terrorists who had been alerted by the sounds of the firefight around the main house.

The Phoenix warriors found themselves confronted by a trio of hard-liners.

Manning's superb reflexes enabled him to engage first, laying down a stream of projectiles from his Uzi. Two of the enemy were deleted in explosions of violence as they tumbled to the ground with numbing finality, their bodies ripped open by the withering fire.

The remaining member of the trio got off an ill-timed burst from his Ingram in the seconds before Katz dispatched him into the next world with a blast from his Uzi. The burning stream of bullets sent the fanatic toppling backward, arms thrown wide in an unwilling gesture of surrender.

Someone opened up from behind the partly open doors of the shed directly in front of Katz and Manning. A trail of slugs scorched the dusty ground, but the Phoenix duo had veered away from the line of fire. Katz darted forward and covered the remaining yards, then flattened himself against the wall of the shed.

Meanwhile Manning found cover behind a stack of rough-sawed timber.

It became clear that the gunner was just inside the door. He released another blast from his concealed position, and the slugs hammered into Manning's woodpile. Katz brought his Uzi into play, triggering a burst at the shadowed hand and arm holding the stuttering SMG just inside the shed's door. The volley chewed the man's hand and wrist to shreds, and the SMG dropped to the ground as its yelling owner fell back inside the shed, trailing blood.

Katz fired again, splintering the doorframe and keeping the terrorists from showing their faces.

Realizing Katz's intention, Gary Manning broke cover and made a run for the building. The Canadian slammed himself against the wall, on the opposite side of the doors from Katz, and raised a thumb to his Israeli partner.

Both men reloaded their weapons in readiness for their next move. Katz reached out and hooked the edge of the door with his prosthesis, then hauled it open. Manning had already pulled the pin on a concussion grenade. He hurled it through the entryway as he and Katz retreated a bit from the wall.

There was a muffled yell from inside the shed an instant before the grenade exploded. Then thick white smoke wisped out through the door.

Moving together, Katz and Manning ducked inside, separating as they entered the spacious well-lit area. The shed had a concrete floor that was taken up by the four Manta units. The false container tops had been removed from the chassis beds to expose the units beneath. The missile covers had been opened to allow access to the missiles themselves. The cab units of the vehicles had been painted white to conceal the original military coloring and identification marks.

A number of men were staggering around clutching their hands to their ears, a very pained look on their faces. Others were down on the floor. Farther toward the back were other terrorists. They had been out of range of the concussion grenade's power, and they were approaching the front of the storage shed.

"Drop your weapons," Katz commanded. "The building is surrounded. Do it now!"

Some of them paused and glanced at one another, as though debating what to do. It seemed that Katz's bluff might work.

"Go to hell!" someone shouted, and the tentative mood was gone. An SMG opened up. Bullets sang their deadly song as they slashed through the air.

"I don't think you got to them," Manning said dryly as he and Katz dived for cover.

"Maybe this will," Katz retorted and opened up with his Uzi, blasting the RBP fanatic who was spraying bullets in his direction. The man went down screaming, but after a brief bout fell silent.

The interior of the building echoed with the sound of autofire and the air seemed to be alive with flying projectiles as Manning crouched beside a steel tool trolley, ducking his head as a stream of slugs whacked against the metal, howling off at all angles. He eased his muscular frame to the opposite side of the trolley, poking the muzzle of his SMG into the open. He picked out his target, a bearded terrorist clad in greasy denims. The fanatic was wild-eyed, mouthing foul obscenities as he advanced in Manning's direction, seemingly determined to blast his way through the steel trolley. Manning quelled that determination with a short burst from his Uzi that thudded into the man's chest, knocking him off his feet. The RBP goon, thrashing around in pain, jerked the trigger of his SMG and sent a last *rat-a-tat* across the floor of the building.

Someone in white overalls was brandishing a Beretta 92-SB as he rushed out from behind one of the Manta units. His brown skin and distinctive features marked him as one of the Libyan technicians brought in to fit the nuclear warheads to the missiles. The Libyan swung his autopistol at Katz, his fingers bearing down on the trigger.

Without warning the Libyan's chest exploded outward, and he was tossed forward, his white overalls drenched in blood. He crashed to the floor, twisting in agony, spilling his blood for the holy war that was over for him.

Katz glanced in the direction the Libyan had been standing and saw Karl Hahn storming across the floor. The German ace was firing as he came, catching the terrorists from behind because he had entered at the back. Using the momentary element of surprise, Katz and Manning opened fire, blasting hot slugs at the confused and disorganized RBP terrorists.

It was Katz himself who took out the second Libyan technician with a well-aimed burst from his Uzi, almost decapitating the man. Caught on the run, the Libyan stopped a storm of skull busters. He fell against the rear wheel of one of the Manta units, then tumbled in a bloody heap on the floor, one hand scrabbling against the hard concrete in a reflex motion preceding death.

Firing over their shoulders as they made a run for the door, a pair of RBP fanatics were stopped in their tracks by Hahn's H&K. His MP-5 rattled an angry burst that chewed bloody holes in the terrorists, sending them facedown on the floor, where they ended their lives as twitching, bleeding things that didn't even sound human.

Katz's next shots got a raging thug in the neck as he jumped out from behind a stack of barrels. He clutched at his ruined throat, but it was over for him so quickly that he died on his feet.

The Uzi in Gary Manning's hands clicked empty directly after he blew away a terrorist tracking in on Karl Hahn. The guy went down in a welter of blood, desperately trying to hold together the hole in his body.

It suddenly became quiet in the huge shed. There were a few moans of pain from the wounded and the dying. The air was heavy with the stench of gunsmoke.

The Phoenix trio stayed alert, weapons tracking back and forth as they moved around the floor. All their senses were fine-tuned for anything that might remotely resemble a threat.

Because of the newly descended silence, the distant crackling of gunfire really got their attention.

"Now who could that be?" Manning asked no one in particular.

"I wonder," Hahn said.

McCARTER HAD EXITED the house by a side door. His eyes searched the area. A helicopter, that was what Harriman had said. It wasn't something easily concealed. Not if you wanted to keep it ready for a quick getaway.

He sprinted along the outside wall of the house, reaching the end of the section that jutted out from the main body of the building. As he broke from cover, finding himself out in the open, McCarter saw the waiting helicopter. It was standing on what had once been a hard-surface tennis court. The chain-link fence that had enclosed the court lay on the ground.

Alex Manson, escorted by two armed terrorists, was making a run for the helicopter.

Just like a rat, McCarter thought. Deserting the sinking ship. At least Manson was running true to form.

The British Phoenix commando tore across the lawn that separated him from Alex Manson. One of Manson's escorts looked back over his shoulder and saw the avenging Briton. He half turned, letting loose a blast from his automatic weapon. The bullets smacked into the grass, well short of their target.

McCarter stopped running and took out his Hi-Power. Assuming a sideways stance, he raised the pistol, aimed and fired. He pulled the trigger twice, sending a couple of missiles through the neck of the guy who had shot at him. The terrorist went down in a tangle of arms and legs, blood squirting from a severed artery. The grass around him was suddenly splotched with bright red.

Manson had raced ahead to reach the helicopter. He yanked open the door, flung himself inside and feverishly began to flick on switches.

McCarter blew away the second escort terrorist as he tried to board the helicopter. The bullet from the Hi-Power crashed through his skull and slammed his head against the Plexiglass canopy of the helicopter. Manson glanced up. He saw the sticky smear left there as the dead man slid down the canopy to the ground.

McCarter jogged toward the helicopter, feeding a fresh magazine into his Ingram, while in the cockpit Alex Manson was desperately trying to coax the helicopter to life. The rotors were beginning to turn, but ever so slowly.

Raising the Ingram, McCarter opened fire. He aimed for the fuel tanks and was rewarded by the sight of liquid jetting from one of the ragged holes in the paneling. He exhausted the magazine. After quickly replacing it, McCarter loosed off more shots into the fuel tank. There was a soft thump of sound as the spilled fuel caught fire. Flames began to show inside the helicopter's body.

McCarter sprinted to the front of the aircraft and stood face-to-face with Alex Manson. The renegade understood at last that he wasn't going to get the machine off the ground and made a grab for the SMG on the seat beside him.

He knew he didn't have a chance when he saw McCarter's Ingram track around and settle on him. The MAC-10 spit flame as the Briton pulled back on the trigger and held it there. The 9 mms shattered the Plexiglas, driving sharp wedges into Manson's body. The combination of slugs and the shards of Plexiglas reduced Alex Manson's body to ribbons of flesh. The deserter was pinned to the back of his seat by the withering blast, his twisted hopes and dreams blown out of existence along with his life.

As the burning fuel boiled out of the ruptured tanks and engulfed the helicopter, McCarter turned away and went looking for the rest of the Phoenix Force. He was halfway to the storage sheds when the burning chopper exploded in a ball of roaring flame that gushed skyward.

The doors of the shed where the Manta units had been concealed swung open. The few surviving RBP terrorists, some wounded, were herded out under the guns of Gary Manning and Karl Hahn. Katz followed close behind.

"How did you manage without me?" McCarter asked as he joined them.

"It was a struggle," Manning replied.

"Is everything all right?" Katz asked.

McCarter nodded, lighting up a Player's cigarette. "Harriman's alive but hurt. The bastards were torturing him. He's going to need medical attention as fast as we can get it for him, but he'll be okay."

"What about Lubichek? Manson?" Katz inquired.

"They took the hard way out," McCarter replied.

Katz nodded. "Let's get up to the house. We'll make contact with Dexter and tell him he can bring in his people to clear this mess up and take charge of the missiles."

"Any indications where they were going to send the missiles?" asked McCarter.

"We didn't get a chance to ask anyone," Hahn said. "Perhaps it will remain a mystery now that all the top men are dead."

Manning shrugged. "Best thing is it didn't happen. Calvin James and Encizo will be happy to know that we, too, held up our end. So we can all go home."

"Mission accomplished," Hahn said.

"Not quite yet for me," McCarter said seriously.

"What do you mean?" Katz asked.

"I came to England for a funeral," McCarter explained. "Before I leave, I've another to attend. One more dead friend. Jake Tasker."

There was silence for a moment.

"You have blood on your shoulder," Hahn said to McCarter. "You must have pulled the stitches in your wound."

McCarter didn't even look. "I hadn't noticed," he said absently. At that moment in time it didn't seem to matter all that much.

Katz looked around thoughtfully. "We did well, though our team was split up. I must say that for the main action we should all be pulling together—it is the best way. We are not many in number, and though we count outstanding talents among us, when the final scene goes down we should turn out full force.'' He chuckled softly at his own joke. ''As in Phoenix Force.''

"Gar Wilson is excellent. Raw action attacks the reader from every page."
—Don Pendleton

SUPER PHOENIX FORCE #1

FIRE STORM

An international peace conference turns into open warfare when terrorists kidnap the American President and the premier of the USSR at a summit meeting. As a last desperate measure, Phoenix Force is brought in—for if demands are not met, a plutonium core device is set to explode.

DON PENDLETON's
MACK BOLAN

FLESH AND BLOOD

California's
Killing Fields

Terror strikes innocent refugees of Southern California's Vietnamese community when they are threatened by the ruthless king of Asia's underworld. Their one and only hope lies with Mack Bolan, and when he challenges the mob, the gangland violence rocks California.

TAKE 'EM NOW

FOLDING SUNGLASSES FROM GOLD EAGLE

Mean up your act with these tough, street-smart shades. Practical, too, because they fold 3 times into a handy, zip-up polyurethane pouch that fits neatly into your pocket. Rugged metal frame. Scratch-resistant acrylic lenses. Best of all, they can be yours for only $6.99.

MAIL YOUR ORDER TODAY.

Send your name, address, and zip code, along with a check or money order for just $6.99 + .75¢ for postage and handling (for a total of $7.74) payable to Gold Eagle Reader Service. (New York and Iowa residents please add applicable sales tax.)

Remove from pouch...

unfold once...

unfold twice...

and they're ready to wear.

GOLD EAGLE

Gold Eagle Reader Service
901 Fuhrmann Blvd.
P.O. Box 1396
Buffalo, N.Y. 14240-1396

GES-1A

Offer not available in Canada.